"I Would Appreciate It If You Would Forget That Night Ever Happened."

A slow grin lifted one corner of his sensual mouth, a mouth that had haunted her for months after their encounter. She still remembered the taste of it, the feel of it on—

"Not likely, darlin'," he said in a slow drawl as he ran a knuckle along her jawline.

Her spine started to soften, then Olivia caught herself and stiffened her resolve. She wasn't going to fall into his trap again. There wasn't room for a man in her plans. Certainly not a man like Jackson.

"Forget it," she snapped. There will never be a repeat performance. Now, if you'll excuse me…" She tried to push past him, but he blocked her way.

"Not so fast," he said, pinning her between his arms and the wall. "Now that I've found you, I'm not about to let you get away…."

Dear Reader,

Celebrate the rites of spring with six new passionate, powerful and provocative love stories from Silhouette Desire!

Reader favorite Anne Marie Winston's *Billionaire Bachelors: Stone*, our March MAN OF THE MONTH, is a classic marriage-of-convenience story, in which an overpowering attraction threatens a platonic arrangement. And don't miss the third title in Desire's glamorous in-line continuity DYNASTIES: THE CONNELLYS, *The Sheikh Takes a Bride* by Caroline Cross, as sparks fly between a sexy-as-sin sheikh and a feisty princess.

In *Wild About a Texan* by Jan Hudson, the heroine falls for a playboy millionaire with a dark secret. *Her Lone Star Protector* by Peggy Moreland continues the TEXAS CATTLEMAN'S CLUB: THE LAST BACHELOR series, as an unlikely love blossoms between a florist and a jaded private eye.

A night of passion produces major complications for a doctor and the social worker now carrying his child in *Dr. Destiny*, the final title in Kristi Gold's miniseries MARRYING AN M.D. And an ex-marine who discovers he's heir to a royal throne must choose between his kingdom and the woman he loves in Kathryn Jensen's *The Secret Prince*.

Kick back, relax and treat yourself to all six of these sexy new Desire romances!

Enjoy!

Joan Marlow Golan

Joan Marlow Golan
Senior Editor, Silhouette Desire

Please address questions and book requests to:
Silhouette Reader Service
U.S.: 3010 Walden Ave., P.O. Box 1325, Buffalo, NY 14269
Canadian: P.O. Box 609, Fort Erie, Ont. L2A 5X3

Wild About a Texan

JAN HUDSON

Silhouette® Desire®

Published by Silhouette Books
America's Publisher of Contemporary Romance

SILHOUETTE BOOKS

ISBN 0-373-76425-1

WILD ABOUT A TEXAN

This edition published by arrangement with Harlequin Books S.A.

Visit Silhouette at www.eHarlequin.com

Printed in U.S.A.

Books by Jan Hudson

Silhouette Desire

In Roared Flint #1035
One Ticket to Texas #1071
Plain Jane's Texan #1229
Wild About a Texan #1425

JAN HUDSON,

a winner of the Romance Writers of America RITA Award, is a native Texan who lives with her husband in historically rich Nacogdoches, the oldest town in Texas. Formerly a licensed psychologist, she taught college psychology for over a decade before becoming a full-time author. Jan loves to write fast-paced stories laced with humor, fantasy and adventure, and with bold characters who reach beyond the mundane and celebrate life.

This one is for all the loyal readers
who have been asking for and eagerly awaiting
Jackson and Olivia's story.

Also, special thanks go to Carolyn Lampman for SSS/IS and
to Buddy Temple, former Texas Railroad Commissioner.

Prologue

He woke suddenly, his heart hammering against his chest. He rolled over and reached for her, but the place where she had lain was empty. Something told him that she was long gone, but Jackson strode through the suite shouting her name. The only sign that she had been there was the second champagne glass beside his on the nightstand.

Cursing, he grabbed the phone and called her room.

"Miss Emory has checked out, sir," the operator told him.

"Checked out? When?"

"I don't know. Would you like the desk?"

"Yeah."

He cursed some more while he waited, turned the air even bluer when he found out that it was ten o'clock in the morning and she had a three-hour head start on him.

Ten o'clock? He never slept that late. Then he remembered that they hadn't done much sleeping the night before. God, he hadn't been able to get enough of her. He'd never met anyone quite like Olivia, never experienced such a powerful connection with any woman. He'd known from the minute he saw her at the first prewedding shindig that she was a special lady. And he'd known that he wasn't the only one aware of the chemistry between Irish Ellison's bridesmaid and Kyle Rutledge's groomsman. Everybody had seemed to notice.

Trouble was, he hadn't been able to get Olivia alone; they had always been surrounded by people—and she had seemed to prefer it that way. In fact, she'd been feisty as a fractious filly when he'd tried to move in on her and cut her from the herd, telling him in no uncertain terms to get lost. But Jackson hadn't let that stop him. God may have shorted him a bit on brains, but he'd made up for it with luck and determination. And Jackson was determined to have Olivia Emory, sass and all.

He had already been making plans to take her back to Texas with him, and damned if she hadn't run off. Well, she wasn't going to get away from him that easy. She couldn't run far enough or fast enough.

Snatching his tuxedo pants from the bedpost, he yanked them on and pulled on his dress boots. He let loose another string of oaths when he couldn't find the studs to his shirt. He grabbed a Dallas Cowboy jersey from a drawer and dragged it over his head as he made for the elevator.

Outside, when Jackson flagged a taxi, he saw that snow was really coming down hard. The cab driver earned his extra twenty bucks, but the few minutes he shaved off the ride to the Akron airport didn't help. Jackson discovered that Olivia's plane had left two hours before he had arrived, and now the runways were shut down. A mean snowstorm was moving in, and all the major airports in the area were closing. He tried to charter a plane or a chopper, but everything was grounded until the storm passed.

The ride back to the hotel was slower, and Jackson felt as if somebody had broken both his ankles and thrown him in a hole. He was miserable. Truth was, he had fallen for Olivia Emory—fallen *hard.*

Strange that he'd zeroed in on her. Even though she was a beautiful woman, she wasn't the type he usually chose. Olivia was a bright lady with a string of letters after her name, and he was dumber than a barrel of horseshoes—coming from a family of smart go-getters, he'd figured that out when he was just a kid. And he'd never cared much for women who played hard to get; there were too many willing ones to put out the effort to chase one.

She was rare. He'd known it instantly.

He had watched her relentlessly the entire weekend of his cousin Kyle's wedding, for, despite her words, he'd known sure as the dickens that she felt the same sparks sizzling between them that he did. Still, she wouldn't even let him hold her close when they danced at the wedding reception. She acted prissier than Miss Culbertson, his third-grade teacher.

They were waltzing with a yard of daylight between them when everything suddenly changed. She started to shake, then plastered herself against him.

"Dance me over to the side door," she'd said. "And let's get out of here."

"Are you sick or something?"

She shook her head.

He didn't question the shift in her attitude again. He chalked it up to his famous good luck—or maybe his charm had finally worn her down. He had danced her to the exit; they left. They found a quiet supper club a few blocks away where they ate and drank champagne and talked.

And laughed. God, how they had laughed. He'd loved the way she laughed, deep and throaty. Sexy as hell. He told every funny story he could think of just to hear the sound of it. Then the banter changed to plain conversation. He couldn't remember when he'd enjoyed just talking to a woman so much.

Back at the hotel, he'd kissed her in the elevator. When the door opened at his floor, they had gone to his suite together as if it were the most natural thing in the world. Making love with her had been unbelievable. Beyond his wildest dreams.

Now she was gone. He was heartsick.

And colder than a well-digger's butt.

It was freezing outside, and it finally dawned on him that he wasn't wearing a coat. Damn, if that woman hadn't turned him inside out!

He hadn't even taken his room key with him. When he stopped by his desk for another, the clerk handed him an envelope.

"What's this?" Jackson asked, frowning.

"A message for you, sir."

Jackson ripped open the envelope and squinted at the contents. The words danced and blurred; he cursed, crushed the paper in his fist and strode to the elevator.

He was going to D.C. even if he had to hire a bulldozer to get there.

One

This is a mistake, Olivia thought as she sat on the back pew of the Dallas church filled with white flowers and wedding guests.

She should never have let her friend Irish talk her into coming to her sister's wedding. Weddings were a jinx. If she had simply driven straight to Austin and not stopped by Irish's house, she wouldn't have been in this predicament. But she had, and she was.

The moment she saw him waiting at the altar with his brother and the others, she'd known that she'd been lying to herself for the past year and a half. Her insides twisted and her throat tightened. The feelings were still there. Just the sight of him churned bittersweet longings deep within her.

Suddenly, the floral fragrance turned cloying, the crowd oppressive. Her survival instincts, honed from years of experience, screamed at her to flee.

Just as she started to rise, the music swelled and every eye turned toward the aisle. Too late. The first bridesmaid appeared in the archway.

Olivia felt her skin prickle, and she knew that he'd spotted her. She tried not to look at him, but her gaze lifted as if responding to a command, and their eyes met. For a moment they stared at each other. Her defenses crumbled; music and people disappeared; time was suspended.

Then he grinned and winked one wicked dark eye. Who else but Jackson Crow would flirt with a woman in the middle of a wedding? He would probably still be flirting with women at his own wedding.

Damn him. Damn his strength, and damn her weakness. And her stupidity for coming today. Another person might offer all sorts of excuses, but Olivia couldn't hide behind the comfort of denial. She was a psychologist—or soon would be. Like the proverbial moth to a flame, she'd come to the wedding because she wanted to see Jackson again.

With tremendous effort, she forced herself to pay attention to the bride's entrance, to the wedding ceremony. Eve Ellison, Irish's younger sister, was exquisite in her simple satin and lace gown. Matt Crow, Jackson's younger brother, looked at his bride with such tenderness that Olivia felt her eyes sting. Irish, radiant with the recent news of her pregnancy, was matron-of-honor, and Dr. Kyle Rutledge, her plastic surgeon husband, was a groomsman.

Despite her best efforts, Olivia heard little of the vows. Her attention vacillated between watching Jackson and glancing anxiously toward the exit. She didn't want to disturb the ceremony by leaving, but she didn't want to face Jackson either. As soon as the church cleared, she would sneak out a side door, take a taxi back to Irish and Kyle's house, and—

Rats! She didn't have a key to the house.

"You may kiss the bride."

She glanced up from the tissue she had shredded in her lap to find the couple in an embrace and Jackson staring at her. She stuffed the shredded scraps into her purse and clutched the small bag with both hands.

"Ladies and gentlemen, may I present Mr. and Mrs. Matthew Crow."

The couple beamed; the crowd stood; laughter and applause broke out. The organ began to play, and the wedding party started down the aisle. As Jackson and Irish approached, Olivia studied one of the stained-glass windows and tried not to hyperventilate.

She waited until every single guest had cleared the pews, then hurried to a side door and flung it open.

There, leaning casually against a wall, stood Jackson Crow.

"Going somewhere, darlin'?"

"I—I'm looking for the ladies' room."

Looking amused, he stepped to one side, revealing the sign on the door behind him. "There it is. I'll wait for you."

"No need," she said with forced gaiety. "I know that you have best-man duties, photographs and such."

"I'll wait."

Once inside, she delayed as long as she could, using cold compresses on her face, then reapplying the lipstick she'd nibbled away during the service. Finally, with no other reasonable options, she straightened her shoulders and opened the door.

A lazy smile broke over his face as his gaze scanned her. "You're a sight for sore eyes. Do you know how long and hard I looked for you after you left Akron in such an all-fired hurry? Where'd you get off to?"

"I went home to Washington."

"I mean after that. I was in D.C. by midnight, and you'd already hightailed it for parts unknown. I did everything but call out the hounds to find you."

"I went to visit a friend in Colorado—not that it's any of your concern."

"Damn right it's my concern. After that night—"

"I'd rather forget that weekend, Jackson. I...I don't know what possessed me to— Well, I'm ordinarily much more sensible. It must have been the champagne. I'm not much of a drinker, and—" Realizing that she was blathering and that he was amused at her discomfort, she stopped and drew a deep breath. "I would appreciate it if you would be a gentleman and forget that night ever happened."

A slow grin lifted one corner of his sensual mouth, a mouth that had haunted her for months after their encounter. She still remembered the taste of it, the feel of it on—

"Not likely, darlin'," he said in a slow drawl as he ran a knuckle along her jawline. "Even though my mama did her best to raise a gentleman, nothing's wrong with my memory."

Her spine started to unravel, then Olivia caught herself and stiffened her resolve. She wasn't going to fall into his trap again. There wasn't room for a man in her plans. Certainly not a man like Jackson. If she hadn't been so terrified when she'd spied her ex-husband across the dance floor, she would never have left with Jackson that night. But she'd been so shocked to realize that Thomas had found her that she'd acted impulsively, thinking only of escape and of Jackson as a heaven-sent protector.

"You might as well forget it," she snapped. "There will never be a repeat performance. Now, if you'll excuse me..." She tried to push past him, but he blocked her way.

"Not so fast," he said, pinning her between his arms and the wall. "Now that I've found you again, darlin', I'm not about to let you get away this time."

A door opened down the hall, and Jackson's grandfather stuck his head out. "Jackson—" He gave a little hoot. "Might have known you'd have a pretty woman cornered somewhere. 'Scuse me, ma'am, but, Jackson, you'd better get in there or your mama's gonna skin you alive."

"I'll be there in a minute, Grandpa Pete."

"Please go ahead," Olivia said.

"I'm afraid if I leave you might cut and run."

Jackson's grandfather, known to everyone as Cherokee Pete, ambled toward them. Well into his eighties, he was still ramrod straight, and merriment danced in his dark eyes. With his long gray braids, he reminded Olivia of Willie Nelson in a tuxedo.

"Well, as I live and breathe," Pete said, "if it isn't Olivia Emory. How are you, young lady?"

She smiled and held out her hand. "It's Olivia Moore now, and I'm fine, Mr. Beamon."

"Moore?" Jackson said sharply. "Are you married?"

"None of that Mr. Beamon stuff," Pete said, both he and Olivia ignoring Jackson's question. "Despite this monkey suit, I'm still just plain Cherokee Pete. Get along, Jackson. I'll take care of Olivia until you're through with the picture taking."

Jackson didn't budge. "Are you married?"

She started to lie. Lying would have solved a multitude of problems, but something in his tone wrung the truth from her. She sighed and shook her head.

"Then why the name change?"

"It's a long story."

"I've got time."

"No, you ain't," Pete said. "Jackson, get going. You can jaw about this later." After Pete shooed his grandson away, he tucked Olivia's arm through his. "Little lady, how about you and me mosey on over to the reception? There's plenty of room in that fancy limousine out front, and I'll be the envy of every man in the room if I show up with such a beautiful woman on my arm. You wouldn't deprive me of that pleasure, now would you?" He patted her hand and smiled in a manner so charming and infectious that she couldn't help but return it.

"You're a shameless flirt, Pete Beamon. Now I know where your grandsons get their charm."

His grin widened and he winked. "Taught 'em everything they know. Come along, Miss Olivia. On the way to that highfalutin restaurant they reserved, you can tell me why your name is Moore now. I'm a mite curious myself. So you didn't get remarried?"

"Not likely. Even though I've been divorced for

three years, I just decided to take back my maiden name.'' That wasn't precisely the truth, but she'd decided that it was the simplest explanation. Actually, Moore was a name she'd picked from a phone book in Durango.

Pete nodded. ''Decided to scrap the name of the sorry scoundrel you got shed of.''

''How did you know my ex-husband was a sorry scoundrel?''

''Just stands to reason. If he amounted to anything, you'd still be married to him. If you ask me, he was a blamed fool to let go of a woman like you.''

If he only *would* let go, Olivia thought as they neared one of the limousines waiting at the curb.

''Glad to know you're single,'' Pete said as he helped her into the car. ''Seems Jackson's taken quite a shine to you, and I've got a proposition to make.''

''A proposition?''

''Yep. Nothing I ever wanted more than for my four grandsons to find a good wife and settle down to raising a family. I was mighty tickled when Kyle hooked up with Irish and when Matt and Eve got together, though both of those pairs had some rough spots, let me tell you. That makes two down and two to go. Now it's about time that Jackson, being the oldest, got himself hitched to that very particular woman he finally found. I can tell he's ready.''

''Ready?'' Olivia felt her chest clutch and her face go warm. ''Who's the very particular woman?''

''Why,'' Pete said, ''you are.''

''Me?'' Her voice went up an octave.

He nodded. ''Irish speaks very highly of you, and I can tell Jackson's taken with you. He was like a bear with a sore paw when he lost track of you. Scoured the woods good for your whereabouts, kept looking for the longest time. Hired a passel of people to help, too. In my book that makes you a special lady. Now, here's my proposition. If you'll marry Jackson, I'll give you two million dollars on your wedding day.''

Dumbstruck, Olivia could only gape at Pete. She knew that the old man, despite his folksy talk and simple ways, was enormously wealthy and could well afford what he was offering. She just couldn't believe that he was actually making the offer. Finally she managed to stammer, ''Two *million* dollars? Ma—*marry* Jackson? *Me?* You're kidding.''

''Nope, I'm dead serious. I just handed Eve her two for marrying Matt.''

''But, Pete, that's ludicrous! I certainly wouldn't marry your grandson for two million dollars.''

The old man sighed. ''Well, truth to tell, Jackson would be a handful for any woman to put up with—not that he's lacking in character, you understand. He's a fine boy. But he's the oldest, and I'd like to see him under the steadying hand of somebody who could see through all his hoorah. It's past time for him to give up his wild ways and settle down. You strike me as the perfect person to tame him, you being a psychologist and all. Irish tells me that you're a real smart lady.''

''Too smart to want to marry Jackson Crow. I'm not interested in taming him, nor am I in the market for a husband, thank you very much.''

"Now don't you decide too quick. Take some time and think about it. It would mean a lot to me to see that boy happy. Why, I'll even up the ante to five million if need be."

Two

Jackson didn't wait for any of the family. As soon as the photographer snapped the last picture, he took off like his tail was on fire. He must have broken every speed limit between the church and the restaurant on Turtle Creek, but he didn't care. He aimed to find Olivia fast. The notion that she might skip out again had him in a cold sweat.

For the life of him, he couldn't figure out why she had affected him so, but something about Olivia had turned him seven ways to sundown. Even after a year and a half, he still thought about her all the time. Maybe he'd built her up into some kind of goddess with no good reason. Maybe if he spent a little time with her he'd find that she was just an ordinary woman, nothing like the person he remembered.

Maybe—

But when he walked into the reception and saw Olivia standing with Grandpa Pete, all the maybes disappeared. Just looking at her made his heart swell in his chest until it hurt, and he felt a big grin spread over his face. Lord, she was beautiful. Long legs, lush body, lips that begged to be kissed and big bedroom eyes that he wanted to dive into.

Beautiful, absolutely. But there was something else about her that grabbed him by the throat, something he couldn't quite define or understand. It was the kind of thing that some people wrote poems about, except he couldn't write a poem if his life depended on it. Every time he was around Olivia, an old memory popped up. She reminded him of a bird he'd once encountered. A blue jay.

When he'd been about ten or eleven years old, he'd received an air rifle for Christmas, something he'd been begging for. He'd half listened to the usual lecture about safety, thinking he knew just what to do. After all, he'd been shooting Scooter Franklin's rifle for nearly a year. Feeling very mature and full of himself, he'd gone into the woods behind Grandpa Pete's store with the rifle and hung a target on a tree.

When the paper bull's-eye had been shot to shreds, he looked around for another target. He tried a few pine cones on a fence post. Easy stuff. That's when he spied the jay. Without half thinking, he took aim and pulled the trigger.

The bird fell to the ground, and Jackson had rushed to view his prey. But the jay wasn't dead; it was only wounded, and it flapped around the ground with a bum wing. Suddenly feeling like a dirty dog for what he'd done, Jackson had tried to pick it up, thinking to take it somewhere for help. The bird wouldn't let him near. It pecked and squawked and fought him until Jackson's hands were bloody and he was in tears. Finally, he'd taken off his shirt and thrown it over the jay to capture it. Held close, it had calmed.

Grandpa Pete had fixed the injured wing and kept the jay in a cage on the porch until it was able to fly again.

Jackson had put the air rifle in the back of his closet and never picked it up again. He never forgot that panicked, injured bird, needing help but instinctively fighting for survival against him.

Olivia had that same fierce way about her, as if *she* were fighting for survival. Had she been badly injured in some way? He was almost sure of it. Everything in him ached to gather her close, to calm her and hold her till she healed.

A crazy notion, he supposed. After all, she was the psychologist. He was just a lucky stiff who had more money than sense and who, to keep from being called a goof-off, built and ran a fancy golf club for his buddies in the millionaires' club.

Still, he wasn't going to let her get away. She might not know it, but she needed him.

He strode toward her.

Play it cool, Crow. Play it cool, he told himself. Don't scare her off.

She looked like a startled doe when he took the wine glass from her fingers and handed it to his grandfather.

"Let's dance," he said, drawing her into his arms.

"There's no music," she said, pushing against his chest. "The band is still setting up."

"I'll hum until they start." He pulled her back to him. "What do you want? Waltz? Fox-trot? Tango? I do a mean tango."

Laughing, she stepped out of his arms. "Jackson, you're still a piece of work. Behave."

He winked. "I'd rather misbehave with you."

"Jackson!" she whispered. "Your grandfather." She gestured with her eyes, indicating someone was behind her.

"Grandpa Pete's gone."

She glanced around. "Where did he go? We were talking."

He shrugged. "No telling. But Pete's sharp. He knows when three's a crowd. If you won't dance with me, would you like a drink? I see that the bar is open."

"Just the wine I didn't get to finish."

"That's easy." He signaled a waiter with a tray of champagne glasses and plucked two from the load he carried. He handed one glass to Olivia.

"Thanks," she said, ducking her head to study the bubbles rather than look at him.

He touched a bit of dark hair at her shoulder, letting the shiny strand curl around his finger. He couldn't help touching her. "You've cut your hair."

She nodded. "Just a little."

"Have you lost weight?"

"Just a little."

He lifted her chin and ran his thumb over the sexy dimple there. "Why did you run away from me?"

"I didn't run away."

"Could have fooled me."

"I didn't run away. I left."

"Why in such a blamed hurry?"

"I explained that in my note. I had to catch my flight home."

"But you didn't stay home. You disappeared off the face of the earth. I know because I looked everywhere for you. Your roommate Kim didn't know where you were. Not even Irish, your best friend, knew where you were. I thought Kyle might strangle me when I interrupted his and Irish's honeymoon trying to find you."

"I told you that I went to visit a friend in Colorado. I had a sudden opportunity for a job, so I went."

"And left no forwarding address?"

She shrugged, then, looking as if she would like to bolt any minute, she chugalugged her champagne.

Back off, Crow, he warned himself. Instead of pressing her, he smiled and held out his untouched glass. "Want another?"

She shook her head.

"Irish didn't tell me you were coming to the wedding. Is this your first time in Texas?"

"I've been in Texas once or twice, and I didn't know about the wedding. I was just passing through Dallas and decided to call Irish and Kyle, and you know Irish. The next thing I knew I was their houseguest and getting dressed for the ceremony."

"Passing through?" he asked, trying to sound casual.

She nodded.

There was a long silence while he waited for her to expand on her comment. Finally he asked, "Going where?"

"To Austin."

"Austin?" He waited again for her to elaborate.

"Yes," was all she said.

Getting information out of her was harder than trying to put socks on a rooster.

"Jackson, my man," a deep voice said as a big hand clamped his shoulder. "Might have known you would try to monopolize this lovely lady. Olivia, it's good to see you again. I'm Mitch Harris. We met at Irish and Kyle's wedding. I understand that you're going to be working with Dr. Jurney at the University of Texas. That's great, really great. Looks like we'll be neighbors. May I be the first to welcome you to our capital?"

Rankled that Mitch seemed to know more about Olivia's plans than he did, Jackson scowled and said, "Get lost, Mitch. This is a private conversation."

Mitch only grinned and shook him playfully by the nape. "Now, Jackson, is that any way to talk to your governor?"

"You're not *my* governor. Hell, I didn't even vote."

And, blast it, Olivia's eyes widened as if she were impressed with the big lug who was standing there looking as smug as a packed-pew preacher.

"Of course I remember you, but I didn't realize that you were the governor," she said, extending her hand to Mitch.

"I wasn't when we met. Hadn't even decided to run then. I was just inaugurated this past January."

"Congratulations, Governor."

Mitch kept holding Olivia's hand a lot longer than necessary, which burned Jackson good. "The only reason Mitch got elected," Jackson said, "was that he used to play a little pro football. People didn't know he got his brains scrambled from all the hits on the field."

"Jackson!" she exclaimed, clearly shocked by his comment.

Mitch only chuckled. "Actually, I think it was mostly because my opponent got caught in a scandal a week before the election. Nobody was more surprised that I was, but I won, fair and square."

"Oh, I'm sure you're being modest," she said.

"No, he's not," Jackson said. "Mitch Harris hasn't got a modest bone in his body. And if you don't get lost, good buddy, I'm going to revoke your golf privileges at Crow's Nest."

"Are you trying to get rid of me?" Mitch asked.

Jackson shot at him with his index finger. "You got it in one, Gov."

Mitch laughed. "Then I guess I'll be moving along. I'll talk to you about that other matter later, Jackson. Olivia, it was good to see you again." He slipped a card from a case in his breast pocket and handed it to her. "Give me a call when you're settled, and I'll show you around, take you to dinner. Austin has some of the greatest restaurants in the state."

If Mitch hadn't walked away right then, Jackson would have decked him. Instead, he jerked the card from her hand, tore it in little pieces and dropped them in a nearby flowerpot.

"Jackson! Why did you do that?"

"Do what?"

"Don't be dense! Why did you tear up Mitch's card?"

"'Cause I don't want you calling him. Stay away from the man. He's dangerous. Let's dance."

She didn't budge. "Dangerous?"

"Yes. He dyes his hair, lies about his golf handicap and wears boxer shorts with little smiley faces all over them."

She tried to keep her lips pressed together, but she finally lost the battle with a laugh. "Jackson, aren't you ever serious?"

"More than you know, darlin'." He pulled her close and breathed in the sweet smell of her. "I'm real serious right now."

"Olivia!" came a feminine squeal from a few feet away.

Olivia pushed away from him, and her face lit up. "Kim!" She held out her arms and they hugged like long lost sisters. "It's been so long. You look great!"

"And so do you. Why didn't you write? We were worried about you."

Olivia shrugged. "Sorry, but you know me. I hate writing letters. It's so wonderful to see you again. Irish tells me that you've had an exciting offer with the state department. Let's go powder our noses and catch up on all the news."

And slick as a whistle, she was gone. Jackson could hardly follow her into the ladies' room—though he considered it. His good manners finally got the upper hand, and he turned away, looking for Mitch. He and his old friend had a little business to discuss.

He hadn't even considered Mitch's outrageous request earlier, knowing that, sure as shootin', he would end up humiliated. He was painfully aware of his limitations. Now things had changed. Jackson told himself that he was letting himself in for a lot of grief, but in spite of the risks, he was going to take Mitch up on his offer. Somehow he would manage to keep from looking like too much of an idiot. After all, he'd been fooling folks for years, and Olivia was worth the gamble.

Olivia and Kim talked nonstop for twenty minutes or more. Finally Kim said, "I hate to leave you, but I promised my folks that I would be right back. Irish invited me over for breakfast tomorrow. We'll spend the morning gabbing." Kim hugged her. "Gosh, I've missed you two." With a wiggle of her fingers, her friend left.

Olivia lingered, repairing her makeup and stalling her return to the reception. She'd loved catching up on all the news with Kim. She'd missed her vivacious young friend. Although Kim was more than a decade younger than Olivia, the two of them, along with Irish, had been housemates in Washington and had become very close. Kim had been in college and working part-time for Congresswoman Ellen Crow O'Hara, Jackson and Matt's older sister and Kim's aunt by marriage. Olivia had been working on her doctorate in psychology and trying to get her life back on track after her divorce. Irish, who had inherited the old house they lived in, was working as a cosmetic consultant and trying to get her life back on track after a terrible mugging in New York that had ruined her modeling career.

The bonds that Olivia forged with the two women had saved her sanity. They had become the sisters she'd never had, the closest thing to a family that she had left. Her mother had died when she was ten. Her older brother had left home the day he turned eighteen, and God only knew where he was. Her father, a prominent cardiologist in Palm Springs, had disinherited her when she divorced Thomas, not that severing ties with her father was any great loss. He was a tyrant whose abuse had driven her mother to suicide, her brother to the streets and her into a terrible marriage to a man who could have been her father's clone.

"Olivia?"

She glanced up to see Irish's beautiful face smiling in the mirror. "Irish, the wedding was lovely. Eve looks so happy."

"She is happy. But you look awfully sad."

Olivia shook her head and tucked her lipstick into her purse. "No, I was just reminiscing about the good times we had in Washington at your old house."

"We did have some crazy times there, didn't we? But come on, the bride and groom are about to cut the cake, and Jackson is wearing a hole in the floor outside. He sent me in after you."

"Irish, I really don't want to get involved with Jackson. I'm simply not ready for any kind of meaningful relationship with a man. I've been stung too many times."

"Oh, don't worry about Jackson. I don't think *meaningful relationship* is in his vocabulary. In fact, someone like him might be good for you. You need to cut loose and have a little fun. Come on."

Olivia had no choice but to rise and rejoin the party.

* * *

Despite her resolve to keep her distance from Jackson, he was at her side almost constantly, and she'd been enjoying herself. He was a wonderful dancer, and she told him so as he whirled her around the floor.

"Thanks," he replied. "I majored in dancing and poker at college."

She laughed. He was such a cutup. "Where did you go to school, and what did you really major in?"

"I have several alma mammies, and my major changed from semester to semester. Academics never interested me the way it did my brother and sister and cousins. I wouldn't have even gone to college if it hadn't been for Grandpa Pete putting the screws to me."

"I recall Irish telling me something about a deal your grandfather made with each of you. He paid for your education, then gave you a million dollars when you graduated?"

"Yep. Then we had five years to double the million. If we did it, he sweetened the pot. My sister sank her million into an ingenious invention by her boyfriend, who's now her husband. Matt started Crow Airline and struck it rich. Kyle made a killing as a plastic surgeon to the stars in California. My cousin Smith, Kyle's younger brother, started a computer company when he was in college and made his fortune."

"And you?" Olivia asked. "How did you double your money? I assume that you did."

"Yep. My biggest talent has always been my luck, so I bought a million dollars worth of lottery tickets."

She stopped dead still, astonished. He did a fast

shuffle to keep from trampling her toes. "*Lottery tickets?* You're joking."

"Nope. If you think about it, I had great odds. Won eleven-million dollars."

"You won?"

"Absolutely."

She shook her head. "Jackson Crow, you're crazy."

He grinned down at her. "Absolutely." He pulled her close and whirled her around the floor again. "I'm crazy about you, Olivia Emory."

She stiffened. "Moore."

"Sorry. Moore. I'm glad you're rid of that bozo's name."

She'd told him the same story about her name change that she'd told his grandfather. Amazing how easily she'd learned to lie, especially when her life had come to depend on it. She had changed names two or three times since she'd last seen Jackson. Her ruse must have worked, for she hadn't seen or heard from Thomas since he'd tracked her to Akron and crashed Irish's wedding reception.

"Relax," Jackson whispered in her ear, drawing her close.

"Pardon?"

"You suddenly went stiff as a post."

"Sorry. I must be getting a bit tired."

"Oh, hell, I'm the one that's sorry. I've been dancing your feet off for an hour. Only way I figured I could hold you and stay decent in front of my mama and daddy. Let's go sit down, and I'll get you something from the buffet. Oh, shoot, Mama's waving at us. You mind visiting with my folks some more?"

"Not at all. I like your parents. They're very nice."

"They're curious is what they are."

"About me? Why?"

"Let's just say that they're sizing you up as a future daughter-in-law."

Her breath caught. "A what?"

He chuckled and kissed her nose. "Don't worry about it, darlin'. I'm a long way from being ready to make that trip down the aisle."

Olivia was cordial with Mr. and Mrs. Crow and chatted amiably with them for a few minutes. She really did like his parents, but when Jackson left for the buffet table, she excused herself politely and stole away. Distance was what she needed. Distance from Jackson Crow. She had no plans to take up with him where they left off in Akron. If she hadn't become so frightened when she'd spotted Thomas across the room, she wouldn't have thrown herself at Jackson and dragged him from the reception.

She retreated to a courtyard outside the elegant inn, a spot lush with tropical plants and hanging baskets. She sat on a stone bench, hoping to make herself invisible behind the ficus tree growing beside the seat.

She felt foolish, a woman hiding like a child to avoid a confrontation, but she'd spent so many years fleeing and hiding, simply to survive, that the response was as conditioned as those of Pavlov's dogs. Instinctively, whenever she felt threatened, she ran.

Jackson Crow posed no physical threat to her—at least she didn't think so. Yet, she seemed to have a penchant for picking abusive men. She'd thought Rick, her college fiancé, was a kind, caring person until the first time he'd lost his temper. And her ex-husband Thomas—

She shuddered.

Olivia had sworn off any sort of significant relationship with men. She didn't have the emotional stamina for it—at least not now. And maybe not ever.

Her brief fling with Jackson had been a mistake, just as she knew that rekindling their affair would be a mistake. She sensed that although Jackson played the clown on the surface, he was a deeply intense individual underneath. The first time their eyes met, she had responded with a visceral feeling that stunned her. The first time he'd kissed her, she'd gone up in flames. The first time they had made love, she'd been lost.

Those feelings were still there.

Jackson Crow was Trouble. She was glad that they would be living over two hundred miles apart.

Holding a heaping plate of food in each hand, Jackson scanned the room.

Mitch Harris strolled up. "Lose something?"

"Yeah." Ignoring Mitch, his gaze scanned the clusters of people again. Where in the dickens had she gone now?

"You thought any more about accepting that appointment to the Railroad Commission?"

"I've had other things on my mind."

Mitch chuckled. "Yeah, I noticed. Beautiful woman."

Jackson glared at his friend. "Keep your mitts off her, Mitch. I mean it. This one is special. If you try to move in on her, I'll break both your legs and all your writin' fingers."

"I got the message earlier, my friend. Jackson, I really wish you'd take that spot for Bledsoe's unexpired term. Things are getting backed up over there. I need to make an appointment this week, and you're my first choice. You're sharp, and I don't know of anybody any more fair-minded than you are."

Jackson snorted. "You're laying it on a little thick, aren't you?"

"No, I'm serious. You know the oil business backward and forward, and I know you keep up with the other areas that the commission regulates. I think you'd be perfect for the job."

"Actually, I have been thinking some about it. I'd have to move to Austin, wouldn't I?"

"Be a devil of a commute if you didn't. Come on, Jackson, it's not permanent—just till the next general election. I know you like Austin, and remember, we've got some fine golf courses in the area."

"None of them as good as Crow's Nest—the first tee is only ten yards from my front door. Austin's golf courses aren't the big drawing card for me."

"Ah," Mitch said, grinning, "but we're soon going to have a drawing card that no place else has. The lovely Olivia."

Jackson answered with a slow grin of his own.

"Tell you what, if you'll agree to take the appointment, I'll show you which way Olivia went."

"Buddy, you're on."

Three

Olivia drove down the tree-lined street on Austin's west side, then turned into the driveway. She bumped over the cracked asphalt that had been heaved upward by live-oak roots and pulled to a stop in her space beside the garage apartment in the rear yard. She waved to Dr. Tessa Jurney, who was sitting on the side porch of the main house.

Grateful to be home and doubly grateful that it was Friday, she climbed from the oven of a car. Sweat trickled from her hairline, and her sleeveless shift stuck to her back from the car's leather seat. She blotted her face and neck with a paper towel from the roll she'd learned to carry with her.

"Come have a glass of iced tea," Tessa called. "You look as if you're about to melt."

"I melted a long time ago," Olivia said as she

walked toward the porch of the two-story house, an elegant white clapboard from the thirties. "Is it always this hot?"

"At this time of year? Always. People around here say that there are two seasons—summer and August. Thank goodness August is finally over. September is a bit better, especially toward the end, and October is glorious." She poured a glass of tea from the pitcher and handed it to Olivia.

Olivia took a long swallow, then rolled the cold glass over her forehead. "The first thing I'm going to do when I get a pay check is to have my car's air conditioner fixed. I never needed it in Colorado, so it wasn't a problem. Even though the car's getting old, it has never given me a moment's trouble. I didn't even know the air conditioner wasn't working until I headed to Texas."

"I'll be happy to loan you money to—"

"No." Olivia held up her hand. "Absolutely not. You and Ed have already done too much for me—helping me get this job and letting me live in your apartment for practically nothing. No loans, but thanks, anyhow."

"At least drive Ed's car for a while. He'll be in Atlanta for ten more days, and it's just sitting idle in the garage."

With the temperatures still soaring into the nineties, it was murder to be stuck in a car without air-conditioning. But Olivia hated to be a mooch. She wasn't accustomed to having to depend on the generosity of others or doing without conveniences—at least not until she left Thomas with nothing but the Lexus she still drove, her clothes and what few personal items she could hurriedly throw into the car. She couldn't even count on her father—he'd disinherited her when she walked out on Thomas, even though she'd been frightened for her life. In the past few years, Olivia had learned to survive on a lot less than she was accustomed to—and been a thousand times more content.

For two years Dr. Tessa Jurney had been her major professor in graduate school at American University in Washington, D.C. Tessa and her family had moved to Texas shortly before Olivia had been forced to flee, but they had kept in touch with a card or a phone call now and then. Tessa and Irish were the only people who knew the whole story—or at least most of it—about her past. Olivia had always meant to finish her doctorate, but with Thomas after her…well, things had gone on hold for a while. Tessa had pulled the strings that had allowed her to complete her degree.

"How are your classes going?" Tessa asked.

"Wonderfully. I have some really bright students in the two undergrad classes I'm teaching, and I'm enjoying my seminar with Dr. Bullock immensely—even though we have lots of reading to do. I just came from three hours in the library."

As Tessa refilled their glasses, a truck stopped in front of the house across the street. The name of a furniture store was scrolled across the side.

"Looks like our new neighbors may be moving in soon," Tessa said.

"Um. Do you know who bought the house?"

"No. Jenny and her friends are hoping that it's a family with a 'really fine' son in her age range."

Jenny was the Jurneys' thirteen-year-old. They also

had a son, Bill, who was sixteen. Both were good kids. Part of Olivia's deal for living in the apartment was to be close by for Jenny and Bill on evenings when the Jurneys went out or the occasional weekend when Tessa and Ed were out of town. Jenny and Bill were at that awkward age when they were too old for sitters and too young to be alone—especially for an entire weekend.

A luxury car pulled to a stop behind the truck and a long-legged blonde got out and hurried up the walk of the Spanish-style home.

"The owner, you think?" Olivia asked.

Tessa shook her head. "Looks like a decorator to me, and I'd venture that no expense has been spared. I priced a chair at that furniture store last year. It cost more than Jenny's braces. The braces won."

The two of them did some more speculating as the delivery men toted couches and tables and chairs up the front walk. In the two and a half weeks that Olivia had been living in Austin, the new-neighbor question had been an ongoing saga. The Sold sign went up the day after Olivia arrived, and there had been a parade of repairmen and plumbers and landscapers coming and going.

It was a beautiful home, Olivia had thought with a tiny twinge of envy as she'd watched the painters apply a coat of warm cream to the stucco. She loved the red tile roof and the sprawling hacienda style with the walled courtyard. A beautiful home indeed, but her little apartment suited her just fine—and she was thankful to have it. Although it was furnished with castoffs as Tessa had warned, the rooms were really quite charming, especially after Olivia had done some painting and spent a couple of weekends scouting garage sales and resale shops. She'd actually enjoyed going "junking" as Tessa called it—and gotten some darned good bargains.

She smiled at the notion of Michelle or Dani or any of her other chichi California pals buying used goods in someone's garage or at a Goodwill shop. Olivia had come a long way from California, and she wouldn't go back for anything. She much preferred the peacefulness of her life now—the friends she'd acquired since she left that life.

"Something amusing?" Tessa asked.

"I was just thinking about how much I like Austin—and going to garage sales. Want to go junking again tomorrow?"

"Can't. Jen has a soccer game that I promised to attend."

Another big truck stopped across the street.

"Moving van," Olivia said. "Looks like Jenny's suspense will soon be over. I hope for her sake that a really fine guy is moving in."

Olivia was brushing her teeth Saturday morning when a knock came at her door. Probably Tessa, she thought. She rinsed and hurried to the door, wiping her hands on the seat of her shorts.

Her heart stumbled when she opened the door. Jackson Crow leaned against the jamb, a big grin on his face and a cup dangling from his index finger.

"Mornin'," he said, tugging the brim of his straw cowboy hat.

"What are you doing here?"

He held out the cup. ''Came to borrow a cup of sugar.''

''Sugar? You came a long way for a cup of sugar. How did you find me?''

''Irish gave me your address. A cute little redhead with braces told me you lived up here. Jenny, I think she said her name was. Say, is that coffee I smell? I'd give fifty dollars for a cup of coffee right now.''

Olivia sighed. ''Okay, come on in, but you can't stay long. I'm going junking.''

''Is that like slumming?''

''Not even close.''

He tossed his hat on the sofa and followed her to the kitchen alcove where she poured a mug of coffee for him. ''Sugar? Cream?''

''One sugar. No cream. Say, this is a nice place you've got here.''

''Thanks. I like it.''

''Cozy,'' he said, standing so close that she could smell the faint scent of his aftershave.

She tried to act casual, as if Jackson's dropping in was an everyday occurrence, but she was so nervous that she spilled sugar all over the cabinet before she finally got a spoonful into the coffee. Why did he have to stand so close? She handed him the mug and stepped back. Unfortunately, the alcove was so small that she bumped into the stove and couldn't retreat any further. His presence filled the compact area as he raised the mug to his mouth and swallowed.

''Ah, that hits the spot. You make a great cup of coffee. You don't happen to have any leftover eggs or a biscuit or something, do you?''

''No,'' she said, yanking open a cupboard, ''but

here's a granola bar. You can take it with you. Now, if you'll excuse me, I have to leave."

"What's the hurry?"

"I told you that I was going junking. If I don't hurry, all the good stuff will be gone before I get there."

"Get where?"

Olivia sighed. "I'm going to hit several garage sales first. I have a list from the paper."

"Garage sales? Well, I'll be darned. You don't strike me as the type." He stuck the granola bar in his pocket, refilled his mug with coffee and said, "Tell you what, I'll go with you." He started for the door, grabbing his hat on the way. "Which one do you want to hit first?"

Olivia tried every way she could think of to dissuade Jackson from accompanying her, but he was unyielding. The last thing in the world she wanted was to spend the morning with Jackson Crow and his extraordinary smile.

Well...not the last thing.

Actually, her spirits had seemed remarkably high from the moment he'd arrived at her door. Just seeing a familiar face, she supposed. But spending time with him wasn't wise. She wasn't going to allow herself to get involved with Jackson. Thank goodness he lived several hours away.

"Why are you here?" she asked as they walked down the steps of her apartment.

"I came to see you—to borrow a cup of sugar."

She rolled her eyes. "No, I mean, why are you in Austin?"

"Business."

"Shouldn't you be tending to it?"

He grinned as he slipped on his sunglasses. "It doesn't start until Monday. I have the whole weekend free. Want me to drive?"

"No, thank you. I'll drive. You navigate." She thrust the folded newspaper and map into his hands and jerked open her car door before he could play the gentleman.

"We're lost!" Olivia said.

"Aw, naw. Why don't you turn left right up here?"

Fuming, she whipped into a convenience-store lot and jerked the newspaper and map from his hands. "We're lost! I thought you were going to navigate."

"I told you that I was better at driving than navigating."

After studying their location and their destination on the map, she realized that they were several blocks away from the garage sale that she'd marked with two stars. "That's where we're going!" She poked a spot on the map. "You've been taking us around in circles." She thrust the papers at him, counted to ten, then pulled out and turned to the right. This was the third time they'd been lost that morning. She could almost believe that Jackson was deliberately trying to make her angry.

"Sorry, sugar," Jackson said, turning his smile up to high. "I'll make it up to you. I'll take you someplace special for lunch. You like Mexican food?"

"I love it, but I'd love finding a desk that I can afford even more. I really need one. Darn it, if we had been there five minutes sooner, I could have bought that one on Elm Street."

''The leg was broken. It wasn't a good deal. We'll find a better one, trust me. At least you got a bargain on that toaster. Two bucks ain't bad.''

She laughed as she pulled to a stop at the address she sought. ''You're the one who got the bargain. I can't believe that you were arguing over fifty cents. Me, I can believe, but *you?* I thought you told me that you'd never been to a garage sale.''

''Haven't. But Grandpa Pete has trading days on the grounds of his store in East Texas. People have been coming to set up tables and booths there for as long as I can remember. They rent space from him and sell everything from used pots to goats. I learned dickering there, learned from a master. No finer horse trader than Grandpa Pete.''

''Seems strange. I thought your grandfather was a millionaire.''

He laughed. ''Billionaire's more like it, but he's just plain folks. We all are. Nothing makes him madder than for one of us to start acting uppity.''

''Uppity?'' She smiled at the old-fashioned term.

''Those are Grandpa Pete's words,'' he said as they climbed from the car and headed for the goods displayed along a driveway.

Olivia spotted it immediately—a small Queen Anne writing table that had been painted a ghastly shade of green. With a little work—no, make that a lot of work—it would be beautiful. And perfect for her apartment.

''Like it?'' Jackson asked.

''I love it,'' she whispered. ''Under that awful paint is a very nice piece of furniture. It's exactly what I've been looking for—better actually.''

"Great. Let's get it."

When she looked at the price tag, she sighed. "I think the owner knows what's underneath the paint. It's sixty-five dollars. Even though it's a steal at that price, I can't afford it. I was hoping to find something for about twenty-five."

"Maybe we can dicker a little."

Jackson knew the outcome before Olivia said a word. Damned if she didn't have tears in her eyes. It about tore his heart out. He'd buy her a hundred ugly green desks if she wanted them, but she was such an independent female, he knew better than to try. He'd found out early in the morning that she didn't intend to take a penny from him, and if he didn't hush about it, she'd turn around and go home right then. He'd kept his mouth shut after that.

But, damn, he hated to see that wistful look on her face as she ran her fingers over the top of the table.

"No go, huh?"

Olivia shook her head. "I could only get her to come down fifteen dollars. You're not considering buying that ratty thing, are you?"

He held up the stuffed armadillo that he'd been looking at to kill time. "I might. I kind of like old Jake here. He has character, don't you think? Grandpa Pete would love him, and he's got a birthday coming up soon. Let me see if I can do a little dickering for him. And these beach towels." He grabbed a couple of towels from the display table. "I saw a lamp over there that you might check out, too."

While Olivia was examining the lamp, Jackson made a quick offer to the plump little woman running the sale. She looked at him kind of funny, but she shrugged and agreed to the deal. He whipped out his wallet, paid her, and made his way back to Olivia with Jake and the towels under his arm.

"Wait till you hear about the package deal I made. Fifty-six dollars for the desk, old Jake, and the towels."

"Fifty-six doll—" She raised an eyebrow and eyed him suspiciously. "Exactly how much was that dreadful animal?"

"Too much. But I made a deal with her—twenty-five for the desk, twenty-five for the armadillo, and six for the towels." He shot her his brightest, most sincere grin. "Grandpa Pete's gonna love this guy."

"Why don't I believe you?"

"Trust me. I know my grandfather's taste. He'll be perfect for his museum display at the trading post. It's full of what you might call *unusual* stuff. My mother says it's beyond tacky."

"Irish told me about your grandfather's place, including the stucco teepee she stayed in. No, I mean that I'm not sure that I believe you got my table for twenty-five dollars."

"Ask the lady," he said with a sweeping gesture toward the seller.

And darned if Olivia didn't do just that.

He could have kissed the garage-sale lady when she said, with a perfectly straight face, "That was our deal. Twenty-five for the desk, twenty-five for the armadillo, six for the towels. You have a way to haul the desk?"

"We'll be back after lunch with my pickup," Jackson told her, scooting Olivia away before she could question the woman further. If he wanted to pay twenty-five dollars for a mangy four-dollar armadillo, well...it wasn't any skin off anybody else's nose.

In the car Olivia insisted on giving him money for the desk. He didn't argue.

"It's hotter'n blue blazes in here," he said. "Crank her up and turn on the air conditioner. How about we get some lunch now? You know how to get to Congress Avenue?"

"Of course. But the air conditioner is broken."

"What's wrong with it?"

"I don't know. I'm going to take it in on the fifteenth and find out."

"Why wait until the fifteenth?"

"Payday."

He bit his tongue and didn't say a word. He wouldn't be surprised if she insisted on paying for her own lunch.

She did.

"Sorry, darlin', but I've got my pride. I invited you to lunch. I pay."

He watched the struggle play at the corners of her beautiful mouth, then she said, "Thank you. The food was great. I loved the tortilla soup."

"Best in town. Austin has some great places to eat. How about dinner tonight?"

"I don't think so, but thank you. Jackson, I really don't want to get involved. I've told you that."

"Involved? You gotta eat, I gotta eat—why not? You have another date?"

She shook her head. "No, and I'm not likely to. I want to start stripping the desk, and I have some reading to do for my classes. I'm very busy. Thank you, but no.''

He didn't plan to give up without a fight, but he let it go for the moment.

Olivia had been completely out of her mind in allowing Jackson Crow within fifty yards of her, certifiable to agree to his accompanying her to the garage sales, completely nuts to go to lunch with him. Driving home with him sitting in the passenger seat was torture. She hadn't forgotten one moment of their night together in Ohio, the way his mouth felt on hers, the way his hands—

''Watch it!''

She skidded to a stop, realizing that she had nearly rear-ended a UPS truck. Her splayed hand slapped her chest, and she sucked in a noisy gasp. ''Oh, dear Lord. I'm sorry. I didn't see him. I didn't see him. I swear I didn't. I'm sorry.''

''No harm done, sugar. Don't worry about it. Want me to drive?''

She shook her head, then eased around the truck. Once past, she stole a glance at Jackson. He was sitting relaxed in the passenger seat, one elbow out the window, one booted foot crossed over his knee, calm as could be. If Thomas had been riding with her, he still would have been cursing her stupidity. And she couldn't imagine Thomas, or any man she'd ever known, spending a Saturday morning going junking with her. And enjoying it.

Yes, it was a good thing that Jackson lived so far away. Even for a woman who had sworn off relationships, a man like him would be hard to resist.

She pulled into the Jurneys' driveway. "Where is your pickup? I don't see it."

"It's in the garage."

She frowned. "Which garage? Is it being repaired?"

"Nope. It's running fine. It's in my garage. Ready to go get the desk?"

"I don't understand. Where is your garage?"

"Over there." He pointed to the house across the street.

Four

"You're living *there?*"

Jackson grinned as he leaned against the side of her car and looked toward his new home. "Yep. Moved in last night."

A sick feeling uncoiled in the pit of her stomach. "But why?"

"Well, the house was ready and the guys had my stuff on the truck, and I have to start work Monday, so it seemed like a good time."

"No, I mean why *there?*"

"I needed a place to live, and it was for sale. I really like the place. Wanna come look around?"

"Jackson Crow, stop being obtuse! Why did you pick a house across the street from where *I* live?"

"Lucky, isn't it? You know I've always been lucky. Did you know that they used to call me Lucky when I was in school?"

"Jackson, don't try to feed me any of that baloney! You didn't just *happen* to buy a house there! You're deliberately trying to make my life miserable."

"Oh, sugar, don't be mad at me. I'll swear on a stack of Bibles a mile high that I never intended to make your life miserable. After I let Mitch talk me into taking a government appointment and agreed to come here, I must have looked at two dozen houses. This was the one I liked the best. Honest. Cross my heart and hope to die." He drew a big *X* across his chest and affected an expression of pure innocence.

She narrowed her eyes. "When did you buy it?"

"Oh, about two or three weeks ago."

"Exactly what date?"

"Hmm, let's see." He stuck his fingers in his back pockets and looked skyward. "Seems to me I signed the papers the day after Matt's wedding. As I recall you were still in Dallas visiting with Irish and Kim. You hadn't even moved to Austin yet. Ready to pick up your desk now?"

She sighed. "I suppose so."

"Good. Let's go get my truck."

He touched the back of her waist to guide her, and she almost jumped out of her skin. Why was it that a hundred men could make such a simple, polite gesture without her even noticing, and yet Jackson's most casual touch could send her soaring?

This was not good.

Living in such close proximity was going to be a problem, but she could hardly order Jackson to move from his house, and she certainly couldn't afford to leave her apartment.

"Look," she said as she strode down the driveway,

"if you're going to be my neighbor, we're going to have to establish some rules here."

"Absolutely, darlin'. You come up with a list, and we'll discuss it later in the week. Say, would you mind stopping by a grocery store with me while we're out? I wasn't kidding about needing sugar. My cupboards are totally bare. I don't even have a jar of peanut butter or a box of Froot Loops in the house."

"Poor baby."

He ignored her sarcasm and flashed that grin again. "I'll bet you don't even eat Froot Loops."

She tried to stay exasperated; she really did. But there was something so endearing about Jackson that her exasperation kept dissolving as fast as she could shore it up.

"What sort of appointment did you accept from Mitch?"

"I'm the newest member of the Texas Railroad Commission. The title is kind of confusing. We don't have much to do with railroads—at least not anymore. Mostly we regulate the oil and gas industry. Three people were elected to head the commission, but one of them got caught with his hand in the cookie jar and resigned. Mitch talked me into filling out his term until the next general election."

"So how long will that be?"

"Oh, a year or so. Isn't that about how long you're gonna be in town?" he asked.

Her eyes narrowed. Was that a smile or a smirk on his lips? "Why can't I believe that this is a coincidence? When did the governor ask you to take the position?"

"About six weeks ago. Long before you came to Texas—though if I'd known you were going to be living in Austin, I'd have already been here to greet you. Want a tour of my house?''

''Maybe some other time. I'd like to pick up the desk and get busy on it. It will have to be stripped.''

''I'll help,'' he said, a slow grin spreading over his face as he gently hooked his arm around her neck. ''Stripping is one of my specialties.''

Olivia scraped the last blob of bubbly green goop from the table and wiped it down with a rag. Under all that paint, she'd found solid walnut. It was going to be beautiful. She dropped the rag on the newspapers layered over a shady section of Tessa's driveway and picked up a steel wool pad to finish the process.

She hesitated a moment in her task, and her eyes went immediately to the male tush in tight jeans sticking out from under her car hood. Make that two taut male tushes. One was Jackson's, the other was Bill Jurney's. Jackson had insisted on tinkering with her air conditioner, and no sooner had he lifted the hood than the teenaged Bill joined him. It must be a male thing Olivia supposed. Jackson and Bill seemed to have bonded already, laughing and talking and taking a trip to the auto parts store for various doodads. Bill, who had obtained his driver's license only a few weeks ago, now practically worshipped the long-legged Texan who seemed to know all about cars.

''I believe that's got it,'' Jackson said. He stood and glanced toward Olivia. When he caught her watching him, he winked. ''I think we fixed it. How's the stripping coming along?''

''I'm almost finished with this step. I still need to stain it. Did you really fix my air conditioner?''

"Think so. Bill, crank her up and let's see if she's cooling now."

After running the engine for a few minutes, Jackson pronounced the job done and closed the hood. Still wiping his hands on a rag, he strolled over to where she worked. "Say, that's looking great. Need any help?"

"You've done more than enough if you've repaired my car and saved me from melting in this Texas heat. Thank you so much. You're a godsend, but I must insist on paying for all the parts you used."

"No problem. Like I told you, it's just being neighborly. The parts didn't come to more than ten dollars, and I had some spare coolant. Bake me a chocolate pie some time, and we'll call it square."

"That's a deal." Of course she'd never baked a chocolate pie in her life, but she could certainly follow a recipe—or buy one from the bakery.

Jackson insisted on helping with the desk, and having two people working did make the staining go faster. He helped her move it into the garage and stayed for the first coat of varnish.

"I can't believe that's the same piece of furniture you got this morning," he said. "It looks real nice."

"I'm pleased with it." She cleaned her tools, then snapped off her rubber gloves and laid them aside. "I'll put another coat of varnish on it tomorrow."

Jackson glanced at his watch. "Looks like I've got just enough time to go clean up before dinner. I'll be back in a shake."

"Oh, I can't go out with you. Tessa has a meeting, and I promised to grill hamburgers with Jenny and Bill and a couple of their friends."

"I know." He winked. "Bill told me. I'm invited, too, and I'm bringing the ice cream."

During the cookout and afterward as they sat in lawn chairs in the backyard, Jackson charmed Bill and Jenny and their friends the same as he charmed everyone else. Jenny and the Dobson twins, Erin and Edie, from down the street were absolutely moon-eyed over him and giggled through the evening as only thirteen-year-old girls can giggle. Bill and his friend Greg glanced at each other and rolled their eyes at the girls' behavior, but they hung on to every word of Jackson's account of camping and white-water rafting in Idaho.

"That's awesome," Greg said.

"Yeah," Bill added. "How old were you when you went the first time?"

"Oh, my brother Matt and my cousin Smith were about your age, maybe a year older. Kyle and I were two or three years older than that, in college as I recall."

"Wow," Bill said, "what a great way to spend the summer."

"Yeah," Jenny added wistfully. "I'd love to go."

"Oh, Jen, get real," her brother said. "You'd be scared to death."

"I would not!"

"Hey, pardners," Jackson said quietly. The squabbling stopped immediately. "Tell you what. We can't go white-water rafting down the Salmon, but we can go tubing down the Guadalupe." He turned to Olivia. "Ever done that?"

"I don't even know what you're talking about, so I suppose I haven't."

Both Greg and the Dobson twins were familiar with tubing, so they explained how you used an inner tube from a truck tire to sit in while the current of the shallow river swept you along.

"It's loads of fun," Erin said. Or was it Edie? Olivia still couldn't tell them apart. "But we haven't been in *ages*."

"We'll all go one weekend soon," Jackson said, "if your parents say it's okay."

"Go where?" Tessa said, joining the group.

"Hi, Tessa," Olivia said. "I didn't hear you drive up. Jackson is promising to take the kids on a tubing trip."

"Only if you go, too," Jackson told her.

"Oh, I don't know about—"

"Please, Olivia," Jenny said. "Please, please, please. It will be such fun!"

When the twins and the boys added their own pleas, Olivia threw up her hands and conceded. "But only if your parents agree."

"I'll agree," Tessa said, beaming.

Olivia shot her a dirty look, but Tessa only beamed wider. From the moment Tessa had met Jackson earlier in the afternoon and heard an abbreviated—and sanitized—version of their past history, Olivia knew that Tessa had matchmaking on her mind.

"We'll see," Olivia said.

"How about next weekend?" Jackson asked to the delight of the kids. "If we wait too long, the season will be over."

"But there are seven of us, eight if Tessa comes."

"Count me out," Tessa said. "I don't swim—or tube, but you can use my SUV."

"No problem," Jackson told her. "I'll have one of the guys bring a van from the club."

"What club?"

"Crow's Nest," Jackson said. "My golf club and lodge in East Texas."

"Crow's Nest?" Tessa said. "I believe my husband Ed has been there on golfing weekends with his company."

Jackson nodded, but didn't comment further.

"Come on, kids," Tessa said, "it's time to break up the party. Bill, would you and Greg walk Erin and Edie home? Night all!" She shepherded Jenny inside, and the others walked away, leaving Olivia and Jackson alone.

"I have to say good-night, as well," Olivia told him. "Thanks again for fixing my car and helping with the desk."

"You're welcome."

She turned to leave, but he fell into step beside her. "I'll walk you to your door."

"It's just up those steps."

"I know, but my mama always told me to see a lady to her door."

The stairs were too narrow to walk abreast, so she led the way, excruciatingly aware of him close behind her. Once on the landing, she turned nervously toward him. "We're here!"

"So I see." He reached up and unscrewed the glaring light bulb.

"Why did—"

"Bugs."

Before she could protest, he kissed her.

His mouth was warm and wonderful, his arms strong and secure.

Pushing him away was difficult. But after a minute or two, she finally found the resolve to do so.

She drew a shuddering breath and said, "That's one of the rules we need to establish. No kissing."

His arms stayed wrapped firmly around her. "No kissing?"

"No kissing."

"Not even a little one like this?" He touched the end of her nose with his lips.

She shook her head.

"Or this?" He pressed his mouth against one eyelid, then the other.

"No."

"What about this?" he whispered beside her ear before his tongue traced the inner shell.

She sucked in a gasp as white-hot flame flared inside her. "Absolutely not!"

"Oh, sugar, I may just die if you won't let me kiss you." He bent and captured her lips once again.

Her knees sagged, and she clung to him, trying to conjure up the resolve that had escaped her once again.

She might have kissed him forever if Jackson hadn't broken it off and said, "Night, darlin'. Sleep tight."

He turned and sauntered down the stairs; she stood welded to the spot, feeling as though she'd been hit by a lightning bolt.

Five

The sun was barely up when Olivia started sanding. She hadn't slept worth a darn all night, so she'd finally given up and gone downstairs to work on the desk. She'd rehearsed exactly what she planned to say to Jackson scores of times, tossing and turning between each version of her speech. While many—if not most—women would be delighted with his attentiveness, she had no intention of being anything other than a friend to him.

There would be no more kissing, no more…anything else. She intended to finish her dissertation, do her internship, then go into practice. Having another man in her life didn't figure into her plans. She had learned her lesson. She intended to be totally self-sufficient and goal oriented.

Despite her determination to disregard Jackson, her gaze kept drifting to the house across the street.

Nothing stirred.

She wiped down the desk with a tack rag and glanced over again. Still nothing.

She was almost finished with the varnishing when Jackson's pickup pulled into his driveway. Where in the world had he been so early?

Not that it was any of her business—nor did she care where he'd been. She directed her focus to the stroke of her brush down the table leg.

"Mornin'," a deep voice said.

Olivia glanced up to find Jackson standing a few feet away. She hadn't even heard his footsteps. The man moved like a wraith, even in boots.

"Good morning," she answered. "You're up early."

"Early? Darlin', I've already played nine holes this morning."

"Of golf?"

"Yep. Promised Mitch. I beat him nine out of nine holes, so he was ready to quit. Tell you the truth, I was glad. I was hoping you'd be up by now. Had breakfast?"

"No, but—"

"Good. Me neither, and my stomach's about stuck to my backbone. Let's go grab a bite at the Magnolia Cafe. They make the best gingerbread pancakes you've ever eaten and omelets that nearly float off the plate."

"I don't think so, but thank you. I'll have a bagel when I'm finished here."

"Looks like you're about done to me. And they have bagels at the Magnolia. They have anything your heart desires, but I never could pass up their gingerbread pancakes.''

She tried to explain she didn't want to make a habit of going places with him, that she didn't want to see him socially and that she didn't plan on kissing him—or doing anything else with him—again. She told him everything that she had rehearsed in great detail during the wee hours of the morning.

He just smiled and said, ''Okay, darlin', if you just want us to be friends, we'll be friends. Come on. I'm starving.''

''But I can't go like this.'' She gestured to her stain-smeared shorts and faded T-shirt. Good heavens, she'd barely run a brush through her hair before she'd gathered it into a rubber band—and she hadn't even considered makeup.

''You look fine to me—and trust me, sugar, you'll fit right in with the Austin crowd. Nobody dresses up much around here.''

''I've noticed that.'' She tried to think of another legitimate excuse, but she couldn't come up with one. And to cap things off, her stomach picked that exact time to rumble.

Jackson chuckled. ''I'll take that for a yes.''

Before she could argue, his hand was under her arm, guiding her down the driveway.

Jackson couldn't help but grin as Olivia polished off the last of her pancakes. God, he was crazy about her. Just being close to her, watching her, made him feel ten sizes bigger. Funniest damn thing—he wanted to laugh and whoop and climb up on the table and crow like a rooster. He'd never felt this way in his life—and been sober. Now he was beginning to understand why Kyle and Matt acted so goofy over Irish and Eve.

Woman-like, she'd been worried about the way she looked, but he thought she looked gorgeous. He liked her dark hair kind of rumpled, and, Lord knows, lipstick and rouge couldn't have made her any more beautiful. Olivia had natural beauty—good bones, lush lips and mysterious eyes that a man could get lost in. Even in her painting clothes, she carried herself with the confidence and grace of a dancer. She oozed sex appeal. Hadn't he noticed a half dozen men watching her as they walked in the café?

Olivia could talk about just being friends all she wanted to, but friendship wasn't what he had in mind for her. He wanted her by his side and in his bed. But he wasn't anybody's fool. He knew not to rush her, sensing that whatever made her skittish was some heavy baggage she carried. Irish had hinted at it but wouldn't tell him the details. Things were going to take some time, and he was determined to be patient—and persistent. He wasn't going anywhere, nor was he going to let her get away again. He would follow her to hell and back. Just call him glue.

He itched to touch her, to stroke her cheek with the back of his hand, to run his thumb along her bottom lip, then lick it to taste the syrup lingering there. But if he did, she'd probably give him another one of those "platonic relationship" lectures. Unable to keep his hands off her another second, he reached across the table and touched her cheek.

She startled.

"Eyelash," he said quickly, smiling.

"Oh. Thank you." She put down her fork and sighed. "I can't believe I ate so much. But you were right. The pancakes were delicious." Glancing around the room, she added, "And you were right. I'm not any more grungy than anyone else."

"Austin is pretty laid-back, and they have some of the best food in the state. We could eat at a different place every meal and not run out of restaurants for a couple of years. Have you ever tried rattlesnake?"

She laughed with that low, throaty sound that rippled his backbone. "No, and I'm not interested in trying it." She laughed again, and her eyes crinkled and sparkled the way he loved—the way he thought of her at night when he couldn't sleep.

"Actually, it's not bad. There's a really great restaurant just outside of town that has excellent exotic game dishes, everything from wild boar to alligator. I'd like to take you one night. We have some fine chili parlors and an Irish pub with food, drinks and music on Sunday nights. We can go there tonight if you want."

She laid her hand across his. "Jackson, didn't you hear a word I said to you earlier?"

He put his other hand over hers. "What was that, darlin'?"

"This…this thing between you and me. It can't go anywhere. I've told you that over and over."

"And what thing is that, darlin'?"

His eyes were riveted on her lips as she licked them. "This…this thing, this feeling…this feeling…"

He leaned forward and said softly, "You mean this feeling that comes over me and makes me want to lay you on the table naked and pour that jug of syrup over your body and lick up every drop?''

Her eyes widened suddenly, and she swallowed. ''Jackson!''

''Sorry, darlin'.''

She jerked her hand away. ''Please stop calling me that. I'm not your *darlin'*. Let's go. We need to discuss this. In private.'' She stood and strode toward the door.

Oh, hell, he thought as he fished for his wallet. He'd torn it now. Why couldn't he have kept his damned mouth shut? Just because he was thinking it, didn't mean he had to say it out loud. He heaved an exasperated sigh, threw a bill on the table and followed her out. Why couldn't she just admit that the chemistry between them was explosive? Anybody with half a brain could tell they were perfect together, and she was smart.

She was also sod-pawing mad. She tore up his pea patch all the way home. He tried to sweet talk her out of her peeve, but his best efforts didn't work. He finally figured that he was better off just to keep his mouth shut and hope that her anger would blow over. For the life of him he couldn't understand why she'd gotten so angry.

Olivia didn't understand why she'd gotten so angry. She had totally overreacted. If she had berated Thomas the way she had torn into Jackson, he would have beaten her senseless. Jackson hadn't even lost his temper. He'd simply said, ''Now, darlin', you're breakin' my heart,'' every time she took a breath.

Oh, come on, Olivia. You've had enough psychol-

ogy to know why you overreacted. It was an ego defense mechanism, pure and simple. The erotic syrup image was more appealing than she was comfortable admitting. He was coming too close, and it was scary. There was no denying that she was very drawn to Jackson, that she enjoyed his company, that she found him incredibly attractive and enormously sexy. That was the problem.

It would be so easy—

No. She wasn't ready to trust a man with her heart again. It had taken a lot of work to get to where she was now; she wasn't going to blow it for another man.

After a quick shower Olivia dressed and grabbed her backpack. She planned to spend several hours in the library doing research.

As she backed out of her driveway, a little red car pulled into the driveway across the street. A very cute blonde, who was at least ten years younger than Olivia and wearing teeny-tiny shorts and a sassy little cropped top went bouncing up to the gate of Jackson's courtyard. She opened the gate and went inside and out of Olivia's sight.

Olivia hesitated for a few moments, fastening her seat belt and adjusting the mirrors, but the blonde didn't make a quick exit.

So much for Jackson's broken heart, she thought as she threw the car into Drive and peeled away.

She muttered all the way to the university library, mostly about male mentality and her stupidity for caring one iota about what Jackson Crow did with his spare time. She *didn't* care, she reminded herself. And, as a matter of fact, if he spent time with Miss

Short Shorts, then he wouldn't be bothering her. Which was just fine.

Just fine.

Finally she settled down and got some research done, reading, making photocopies of articles and checking out a tall stack of books. By the time she lugged her material to her car and drove home, the sun was hanging low over the tree-covered limestone hills.

The little red car was still in Jackson's driveway.

Damn!

No, scratch that. She didn't care. Not one single bit.

Chin high, she wheeled into her parking space, gathered her stuff and slammed the car door behind her. She stomped up the steps to her apartment, dumped her belongings on the couch and went directly to the kitchen sink. She didn't go there because the window afforded a perfect view of the tile-roofed hacienda; she went there because she was thirsty. She drank two glasses of water, very slowly, then dusted the sink with scouring powder and began to scrub the shiny porcelain.

Her fingers were beginning to pucker when Miss Hot Pants bounced through the gate. Jackson sauntered along after her, and the two of them were laughing. When they reached the little red car, the blonde turned, tiptoed and kissed Jackson on the cheek.

Olivia slammed the sponge in the sink and stalked off. With her tiny apartment, she didn't have much stalking room, so she opted for a shower.

As he always did after one of those marathon sessions, Jackson had a splitting headache. He took a couple of aspirin and rocked back in his recliner to let them take effect. He dozed for a few minutes, and when he woke after about half an hour, he felt better. He washed his face and hightailed it across the street to Olivia's apartment.

On his way he checked the desk in the garage and found that the varnish was dry. He carried it upstairs and set it on the landing.

When he knocked on her door, she didn't open it. Instead, he heard a muffled acknowledgment from the other side.

"Hey, darlin', it's Jackson. Want to grab a hotdog and go to a movie?"

She opened the door a crack, and he tried to go inside, but the screen door was latched. He couldn't see much of her, but it looked as if she had a towel or something wrapped around her head.

"I'm sorry, but no. I'm conditioning my hair, and I have to make preparations for my classes tomorrow."

"How about I go pick up some barbecue or get some Chinese takeout? You've got to have dinner."

"No, thank you." And damned if she didn't slam the door in his face.

He knocked on the door again.

She didn't answer.

"I brought your desk up," he yelled.

After a long pause, the door opened again. "That wasn't necessary."

"I know that it wasn't necessary, but it's too heavy for you to be struggling with. Unlatch the screen, and I'll bring it in."

She didn't look too happy about it, but she did as he asked and stood back as he carried the writing desk inside.

"Where do you want this?"

"There by the window."

He positioned the desk and stepped back. "You know, it looks great. You did a fine job with that old green castoff we bought. I never would have thought something so pretty could be under all that ugly paint."

"Thank you."

"Glad to oblige."

He hadn't missed that she was wearing a robe, and she clutched the front of it primly to her throat. She smelled like bubble gum and wildflowers.

"Sure I can't talk you into some barbecue? Some ribs would really be good. Or maybe some brisket. I really hate to eat by myself."

"Perhaps Miss Hot Pants will go with you."

He frowned. "Miss Hot Pants?"

"The bouncy little blonde in the cropped top that you spent the afternoon with."

"Bouncy—you mean Tami?"

"Yes, I suppose her name would be Tami. Or Tiffany."

He laughed. By damn, if he didn't know better, he'd think Olivia was jealous. Well, well, well. He considered stringing her along for a while, but he decided not to chance it. The truth always worked best. "Sugar, Tami is one of my assistants."

"Assistants? She doesn't look much older than Bill Jurney—not that I had more than a glance at her. I mean, I just happened to see her arrive as I was leaving. She's very…cute.''

''Yes, she is cute. And smart as a whip. So's Paulie.''

''Who's Paulie?''

''Tami's little boy. Hers and Jimmy's. He's almost three.''

''Jimmy?''

''No, Paulie. I think Jimmy is about twenty-four.''

''Wait a minute,'' Olivia said. ''Who is Jimmy?''

''Jimmy is Tami's husband. They've both worked for me at Crow's Nest for years. Tami's daddy and I go way back. They were real tickled when I took the appointment here. Jimmy graduated from the local junior college last May, and now he's going to take classes at UT. He plans on being a vet.''

''I see.''

Was he imagining it, or did her face soften after he explained who Tami was? No, there was a definite softening. ''Can I convince you to change your mind about the barbecue?''

''No, I'm having soup. I was preparing it when you banged on the door.''

''What kind?''

''Chicken noodle.''

He grinned. ''Great. That's my favorite. I'll eat with you.''

''But…but it's only canned soup.''

''I love canned soup. Long noodles or round?''

''Long.''

''Perfect. Where are the crackers?''

Six

Olivia tried every excuse she could think of to get out of going tubing with Jackson and the kids, but between Jackson, Jenny and, of all people, Cherokee Pete, she finally conceded defeat. Buddy, a young man who worked at Crow's Nest, had brought a minibus from the East Texas lodge on Friday evening, and Jackson's grandfather had come along for the ride.

"Wanted to see your new house," Pete had told his grandson. "Besides, I couldn't miss a chance at tubing." He'd even talked Tessa into joining them.

On Saturday morning, after Jen's early soccer game, the five adults and five kids piled into the minibus with their gear and drove to New Braunfels. The route through the hill country was breathtaking with its craggy limestone hills, still lush with cedar and small oak trees that covered the rises like mounds of green tufted pillows.

Olivia sat next to a window with Jackson beside her, his arm casually draped across the back of her seat. He commented on various points of interest as they rode, but for the life of her, she couldn't concentrate. He was very close.

She could smell his aftershave and feel the warmth of his body as he leaned across her to gesture toward some site or the other. He was so close that she could almost count his eyelashes, and she noted the laugh lines that radiated from the corner of his eyes.

He caught her watching him and winked. She quickly turned her attention back to the scenery. He didn't say anything, and neither did she, but the air between them vibrated with awareness. She was relieved when Jen and the twins got everyone involved in a game of twenty questions.

In an hour they arrived at the river where they rented inner tubes. Buddy took care of the rental details, and soon they were in the river, all wearing bathing suits and T-shirts and sneakers to protect their feet from the rocky shallows. Even Jackson traded his boots for well-worn sneakers.

Olivia had never had so much fun in her life. They drifted down the shallow stretch, sometimes slowly, sometimes at a faster clip, paddling around rocks and shouting to one another. They sang silly songs and laughed and splashed until they landed on a sand bar, then they hoisted the tubes and walked upriver to begin the trip again.

Cherokee Pete, at eighty-plus, stayed in the thick of things, and when they stopped for a picnic lunch, the kids gathered around the old man like bees to a honey pot.

Olivia stretched out on a quilt to allow her lunch to settle and listened to Pete's endless supply of tales—which captivated her as much as it did the young people. Jackson dropped down beside her, casually eased her head onto his thigh, then sat sipping the last of his soft drink and twirling a wildflower between his fingers.

''Having fun?'' he asked.

''Umm,'' she managed to answer, her eyes closing. Feeling totally relaxed for the first time since she couldn't remember when, a delicious languor stole over her, and she wanted to drift in that peace forever.

Distant laughter, the river's rush, a balmy day and the smells of water and grass and mustard lulled her deeper. The company of Jackson and his grandfather and the others brought a comforting sense of security that wrapped her like a down bunting.

The kids left first, Buddy going with them to supervise. His grandfather glanced at the sleeping Olivia, smiled, then rose and headed for the river. Tessa winked at Jackson, then she, too, stood and left.

Jackson didn't have the heart to wake her, wouldn't have for the world. She looked as peaceful and trusting as a child, sleeping with her head on his lap. He hadn't realized how strained her face always looked until he saw it relaxed. He wondered for the umpteenth time exactly what it was that dogged her so.

Deep feelings for her began to stir inside him, catching at his chest and his throat. She sighed, shifted slightly and slipped her hand under her cheek and atop his fly—or where his fly would have been if he'd been wearing jeans instead of a flimsy bathing suit. His feelings weren't the only thing that was beginning to stir.

He silently muttered a colorful curse and tried to get his mind on something else, but his mind went back like an oiled gate hinge. Things got progressively harder.

Caught somewhere between heaven and hell, Jackson endured. He sat there and endured, sat there with his sword and held off the dragon while she slept.

The following afternoon Cherokee Pete knocked on Olivia's door while she was engrossed in lecture notes for her classes.

"Come in," Olivia said, holding open the screen door. "I was just about to stop for a glass of tea. I hope you'll join me."

"Don't mind if I do, Miss Olivia," he said, stepping inside and looking around. "Right pretty place you have here. Yessiree, right pretty. I like that rocking chair. Puts me in mind of one my wife used to have."

"Thanks. I found it in a junk shop and refinished it."

His gnarled fingers stroked the carving on the high back, then set the chair to rocking. "Did a good job. My wife was handy at that kind of thing, too."

"Has she been gone long?"

He sighed. "More years than I like to remember. Say, I was hoping you wouldn't mind an old codger interrupting your afternoon for a little bit. Jackson and Tami were working on commission business, and Buddy went to visit with Tami's husband, Jimmy. I've already finished the murder mystery I brought with me, and Jackson doesn't have a blamed thing in the house to read except cases coming before the Railroad Commission tomorrow."

"If you're looking for something to read, you're welcome to look through my bookshelves. I like mysteries, too, and I've picked up several at garage sales lately. Seems like anywhere I land I start collecting books."

"Me, too," Pete said, "and I'm much obliged for the offer. I could go to the bookstore, but Buddy took Jackson's pickup, and I wasn't too keen on trying to drive the bus or that fancy foreign job of Jackson's, especially since I'm not too familiar with the town."

"Would you like for me to drive you to the bookstore?"

"Oh, no," Pete said, squatting to look at the titles on the lower shelf. "I see two or three here that I haven't read—if you don't mind me borrowing them." He selected two books by Mary Willis Walker, an Austin mystery writer Olivia had recently discovered.

"Those are excellent. I think you'll enjoy them."

He also picked up a title by psychologist Carl Jung and thumbed through it. "I'm right fond of Jung. I haven't read any of his stuff in a while. I'm gonna do that when I get back home."

Olivia tried to hide her shock, but it must have shown, for Pete chuckled. "Surprised that an old coot like me reads books by psychologists?"

She smiled. "A little bit, I suppose. Sorry."

"No need to be sorry. Most people are shocked out of their gourds when they see my library at home. My wife—she was a schoolteacher, you know—well, she taught me to read and taught me a love of books that has endured for over sixty years. I read purt-near everything."

"I'm impressed. I love books, too."

"Speaks well for your character. I didn't have much in the way of formal education, but I put a high price on it. That's why I dangled a carrot for my grandkids to go to college. They were all good students, too. Well," he said, chuckling, "'cept for Jackson. He never cared much for books and schooling—had his mind on other things—but he kept on until he got that college degree.

"Always seemed peculiar to me. Of all my grandchildren, Jackson's the smartest of the lot, smarter even than Smith, and he's a whiz, let me tell you. You haven't met Smith, have you? He's into making computers. Lives down in the Valley and grows cotton and citrus fruit, too."

"You're very proud of your grandchildren, aren't you?" Olivia asked, smiling at the old man's preening comments.

"That I am. Shows, does it?" He laughed and slapped his thigh. "I've been real blessed. I have two fine daughters, five outstanding grandchildren, and two super-duper great-grandchildren—with another on the way."

"Let's have that tea, and you can tell me about those super-duper great-grandchildren."

He smiled broadly. "I don't take much prodding to run off at the mouth. And, say, before I forget it, I've got a big pot of chili simmering on the stove, and you're invited to supper. I won't take no for an answer."

"Then I suppose that I'll just have to say yes."

"While you're in such an agreeable mood, young lady, how about taking me up on that other offer I made?"

Olivia frowned. "Which offer?"

A mischievous sparkle lit his eyes. "The one where I give you five million to marry Jackson."

"Forget it, Pete. Not even for you would I get married again. Do you like lemon in your tea?"

Olivia couldn't believe how quickly the weeks passed. Perhaps it was because her life was full and she was content, but before she knew it, September was gone and October was almost over. The last Saturday in the month dawned with a bit of crispness in the air—still warm, but with a definite hint of fall. Olivia threw open the windows of her apartment and was about to make a bowl of cereal when she heard a scratching at her door.

She opened it, expecting to see Jackson with another invitation to breakfast or to the movies or to some other event. No one was there.

Then she looked down. A puppy sat on the landing, an envelope in its mouth. "Well, hello there, little fella," she said, scooping up the ball of brown and white fluff into her arms. "What have you here?"

She tried to take the envelope from his mouth, but he wouldn't let go. He growled a little puppy growl and shook his head from side to side in a tugging game.

"Hey, Sport," Jackson said from a spot halfway down the stairs, "you're supposed to deliver it to the lady, not mangle it." He grinned up at Olivia. "Sorry.

We practiced and practiced, but he's young yet. The only thing he has down pat is eating and piddling on the carpet."

"He's adorable. What kind is he, and where did you get him?"

"What kind? Who knows? I believe that his mama was a golden retriever and his papa was a champion fence jumper. I got him at the SPCA. Jimmy works there part-time, and he and Tami talked me into it. Tami is a one-woman adoption agency for the commission. Everybody in the building will have a new pet before she's finished. Want a kitten? Or maybe a goat?"

"No, thanks. I don't think Tessa would appreciate it."

"I don't think Mrs. Lopez is too thrilled about Rowdy here, either." Mrs. Lopez was the housekeeper Jackson had hired a few weeks before. "He hasn't quite gotten the hang of indoor living, and she banished both of us while the kitchen floor dries. Want to go to Zilker Park with us?"

"I was just about to have some cereal."

"Poured the milk yet?"

"No."

"Good. Dump it back in the box, and we'll stop for a sausage biscuit and orange juice. I want to try out my new kite."

"Your *kite?*"

"Yep. It's a fine one."

He wore his customary boots and sunglasses along with well-worn jeans, straw hat and a T-shirt extolling the virtues of a popular beer. He looked better outfitted for horseback riding or bar hopping than a romp in the park. "Somehow I can't picture you flying a kite."

"Oh, sure. Matt and my cousins and I used to spend most of the summer making and flying kites. We got pretty good at it. My new one is professionally made—a black bat wing with dual controls. Matt sent it to me for my birthday."

"Is *today* your birthday?" she asked, feeling terrible that she hadn't even bought him a card.

"Nope. Tomorrow. Come on. Let's go to the park."

She hesitated. It seemed that they were spending more and more time together—most weekends and several times during the week they went out to dinner or to a movie or to a play that Jackson had tickets for. She always enjoyed herself, but she planned to pass the current weekend alone for a change.

"Sorry, but I want to go to the bookstore and do some browsing this morning."

"Tell you what. Let's go to the park for a while, then we'll drop Roscoe here off, have some lunch and spend the afternoon browsing in the bookstore."

"I thought the puppy's name was Rowdy."

"I haven't decided on a name yet. I'm trying out different ones to see which one fits best."

"That may be part of your problem in training him. The poor thing is confused."

"Ach, an identity crisis you sink, Frau Freud?" Jackson asked in a terrible German accent.

"I sink," she said, laughing, "that you'd better stick to English."

"I'll have you know, darlin', that I had four years of Spanish and four years of French in college." He grinned. "'Course I only got credit for two of each. Come on, *cheri,* we're burning daylight."

As usual, Olivia ended up going with him. After all, she thought, making another in her endless list of excuses to herself, tomorrow was his birthday. And nobody could make her laugh and feel quite as carefree as Jackson Crow.

And nobody could make her feel quite as safe—or quite as vulnerable—as Jackson Crow.

At the park, before Jackson could slip the new leash on, the puppy barked and took off after a butterfly. Yelling didn't stop the determined little fellow, so Jackson went one way and Olivia the other, trying to corral him. Every time they were about to pounce, the puppy, thinking it was a grand game, slipped through their legs and shot off in the opposite direction.

"That little dickens is like a streak of greased lightning," Jackson said as he ran after the scamp. "Try to cut him off at the tree."

They chased him for a quarter hour until Jackson finally caught him by the scruff of the neck and fell laughing into the tall grass of the field. "Lord, I'm worn out," he said, rolling onto his back and holding the wiggling dog on his chest. "How about you, Streak?" he asked the puppy.

The puppy yapped and wagged his tail.

Olivia laughed as she dropped down cross-legged beside them. "I think you may have named him. How about it, Streak?"

The puppy yapped again and licked Jackson's nose.

"Streak it is," Jackson said, slipping the leash on. "I think I'm too tuckered to fly my kite."

"Absolutely not!" Olivia said, hopping to her feet "I want to see it."

They went back to the truck, retrieved the kite and Olivia held Streak's leash while Jackson got the big black bat wing into the air.

It was a glorious thing looping and diving and swirling high in the air. Jackson was very adept, and she enjoyed watching him put the kite through various tricky maneuvers. She also enjoyed watching the man—watching how his arms and back and shoulders moved with the strength and grace of a big cat. How familiar those arms had become.

How often, like now, she ached to have them around her. No matter how many times she told herself to keep her distance, she discovered that all those warnings were futile. The plain fact was she was attracted to Jackson Crow. She enjoyed his company. Why shouldn't she let him hold her or kiss her? She was a mature woman with needs. He was a mature man with needs. Perhaps they could have a relationship of sorts. Such an arrangement didn't have to mean a lifetime commitment. It wasn't as if she planned to marry him, for heaven sakes.

Hmm. She was going to have to give this some thought.

"Want to try it?" Jackson asked.

She almost blushed, then realized that he was talking about flying the kite. "Sure. Why not? What do I do?"

She tied the puppy to a signpost, then, standing between Jackson's outspread feet, took the controls. With her back against his chest and his arms pressed against the outsides of hers, he guided her. In tandem, almost as one, they stood while the kite tugged at the strings, strained at the controls as if it wanted to break free and soar to the clouds and beyond. It danced on the currents and dove with a pull of the cord, yet its goal seemed to be to snap the restraints and fly untethered to the top of the world.

For some strange reason, tears clogged her throat for a heartbeat. Silly, she told herself, that a kite could move her to such sentimentality, but at that moment she felt an overwhelming kinship with it.

And with Jackson.

As if they were one. Their arms and bodies continued to move in perfect synchronization.

Perfect.

They were perfect together.

Perfect.

From nowhere, panic rushed in and flooded her body. She struggled in his arms, stepping on his foot in her haste to get away from him, from the power of the moment.

"Ouch! Whoa, sugar," Jackson said, grabbing for the controls. "What's wrong?"

"Let me go. I can't breathe." She struggled wildly.

"Hang on a second." He nosedived the kite and dropped the strings. He grabbed her upper arms and faced her to him. "What's happening? What can I do?"

"Nothing," she said, splaying one hand across her heaving chest and pushing him back with the other. "Give me a minute." She turned, walked away and sucked in several deep breaths.

As she began to calm herself with a familiar ritual,

she felt like a damned fool. She hadn't had a panic attack in ages.

"Honey?" Jackson's voice sounded worried.

She made a big show of coughing and patting her chest before she turned around. She took another big breath, then pasted on a smile. "Sorry. Allergies. Must be something blooming around here that disagrees with me. For a moment there something took my breath away—literally."

"Do you need to go to a doctor—or to the emergency room?"

"Heavens, no. I have some pills in my apartment." That part was true. She had some antihistamines that the doctor had given her for problems caused by the terrible cedar pollen.

"Let's go get you one." He grabbed her elbow and started propelling her to the pickup.

"Hold on," she said. "It's not critical. We can't leave Streak and the kite. I'll get the puppy while you wind up the kite."

On the way home, Olivia had to caution Jackson twice to slow down. Realizing the extent of his concern, she felt terrible for fibbing to him. But she would have felt worse having to admit her anxiety. As a soon-to-be psychologist, she felt absolutely stupid for being prey to her emotions. In her head she knew that Jackson was a very different kind of man than Thomas or her father. She didn't feel threatened by him—especially after having gotten to know him over the past several weeks. But emotions didn't have brains, they weren't ruled by reason or logic. Propelled by the past, they sped directly from the unconscious to the nerve endings.

She was sure that she'd gotten over most of her anxiety, but obviously a lot of old baggage remained inside her, hanging around to give her grief if she strayed too far from safety. Therapy had been helpful but time often was the best healer.

Obviously, she wasn't ready to trust Jackson yet. A relationship with him was still too threatening.

Back at her apartment, Jackson insisted on coming inside while she took her medication. There was nothing to do but continue her charade.

Oh, what a tangled web we weave… she thought as she unlocked her door.

Jackson picked up the envelope that Streak had mangled earlier. "I forgot to tell you," he said, "that we're invited to the governor's mansion for a reception. This is the invitation. It's in three weeks."

"What's the occasion?" she asked over her shoulder as she headed for the kitchen alcove.

"Meeting the president and the first lady."

"You're kidding, right?"

"Nope. It's for real. Wanna go rub elbows with the movers and shakers?"

Her first inclination was to say no, but who refused an invitation like that? "I'd love to meet the president and the first lady." She picked up the medicine bottle on the counter and turned to Jackson. "I don't think I need this after all, I'm feeling much better now."

"Then we need to stay inside. No pill, no bookstore."

She took the blasted pill.

Seven

"I love this place," Olivia said as they walked into the large bookstore. She took a deep breath and savored the distinctive scent of pristine pages and new bindings. "Don't you love the way it smells?"

"Sure do," Jackson said. "Want a cup?"

She glanced at him and frowned. "Pardon?"

"Want a cup of coffee?"

When she caught the subtle aroma of coffee from the bar to the side of the huge area, she understood his question. "Not now. I was talking about the way the bookstore smells, better even than libraries. Libraries smell like history and tradition, and bookstores like this one smell like new beginnings. I love the scent of books, new or old."

"I guess I never paid much attention. Are you looking for anything special?"

She shook her head. "I thought I would check out the new arrivals, then browse the bargain tables. How about you? Interested in anything particular? We've never talked much about our favorite authors. Who's yours?"

"Oh, uh, I have several," he said. "What about you?"

She smiled. "Me, too. My list is endless. For fun I like to read mysteries or romantic comedies. What about you? What are some of your favorite books?"

"Well, let's see. Uh…uh, I like mysteries, too. And Westerns. I like Westerns a lot."

"Don't tell me. I'll bet you like Louis L'Amour." She grinned.

"He's not bad. Let's see, uh, I liked *Lonesome Dove*."

"McMurtry's great, isn't he? You know, I think he has a new book out. Want to check? You need to start filling up all those bookshelves in your den. Why don't we split up, and I'll meet you at the coffee bar in half an hour or so."

"Sounds good to me."

Jackson waited until Olivia disappeared behind the stacks before he hurried to the information desk in the center of the store. What on earth had possessed him to come to this place with her? He must have been nuts. He'd sooner walk barefoot through a field of grass burrs than to set foot in a bookstore—or a library. Being around all these books made him edgy. He shook his head. Of all people, he *would* have to fall head over heels with a book lover. Go figure.

At the information table, he eased over to a kid

with a badge on his chest and said quietly, ''Say, I need some help.''

''Yes, sir. What can I do for you?'' His words seemed to reverberate through the store.

''Shhhh. Keep it down.'' Jackson glanced around to see if he could spot Olivia. He couldn't. ''I want to buy some books, and I need help,'' he said softly. ''I want a lot of books—in a hurry.''

''What kind do you want?'' the young guy whispered.

Jackson glanced over his should again, then said, ''I want everything you've got by L'Amour and McMurtry, all the latest bestsellers, ten or twelve of your best new mysteries, and, oh, some romantic comedies.''

Jackson had to hand it to the kid. His eyebrows barely moved. ''Yes, sir. The bestsellers, do you want fiction or nonfiction?''

''Both.''

''Hardback or paperback?''

''Hardback. And there's an extra fifty in it for you if you can help me gather them up in twenty minutes and keep quiet about helping me.''

''Let's take a buggy.''

The kid grabbed a cart and took off toward the back of the store like a prairie fire with a tailwind. Jackson took off after him. They stopped at a large display.

''These are the latest bestsellers,'' the kid said out of the side of his mouth. ''Want one of each?''

''Yeah.''

The kid grabbed one from each pile, dumped them in the cart, then took a hard right and went up two aisles. ''McMurtry,'' he whispered. He pulled several books and added them to the rest. "Let's get L'Amour, then we'll tackle the mysteries."

They hurried down the center aisle, the kid steering the buggy like a speed demon. They stopped at another shelf, and his helper frowned.

"Something wrong?" Jackson asked.

"Well, most of our L'Amour are paperbacks. That and tapes."

"Tapes?"

"Yeah, you know, like cassette tapes for when you're driving your car. We have a couple of his big collections on tape."

"Tapes?" Jackson grinned. "Well, what do you know. Tell you what, I'll take whatever you've got, hardbacks, paperbacks and all the tapes. Have you got McMurtry on tape too?"

"Oh, yeah. Grisham, too."

"Who's Grisham?"

The kid picked up a book from the buggy and flipped it over to the author picture. "Him."

"Oh, *that* Grisham," he said, not recognizing the man from a walleyed calf. "I want tapes of every book here."

"Not all of them are available on tape."

"I want the ones that are," Jackson said.

"We're gonna have to hurry if we want to beat the deadline and get tapes, too."

"I'll give you an extra five minutes and an extra fifty bucks."

"You're on." The kid burned rubber on the buggy.

They had a close call once—almost ran smack into Olivia—but Jackson managed to grab the kid and duck behind a display of calendars before she saw them.

Jackson had to hand it to the clerk, he was as fast as a dust devil. In half an hour the cart was jam-packed with merchandise. He slipped the boy a hundred and wheeled his stuff to the checkout stand.

The cashier eyed the loaded buggy, then smiled. "You must really like to read," she said.

"If you only knew," Jackson said, stacking the volumes on the counter.

After he paid for his purchases, he took the three shopping bags full of books and tapes and went to the coffee bar. He was on his second cup when Olivia appeared.

"Sorry," she said. "I lost track of the time. I do that when I get around books."

"No problem. Want a cup of coffee?"

"I think I'll have an iced cappuccino instead."

"You got it, sugar." He rose and went to the counter.

When he returned with her cappuccino, she was peering into one of his shopping bags that was sitting on the floor.

"You bought *all* these?"

"Yep. You said my shelves needed filling. I figured this was a start."

She picked up a book on top and frowned. "Why on earth did you buy a book on menopause?"

Jackson damned near dropped the cup. "It's, uh, for Mrs. Lopez."

She looked at him strangely. "Do you think she reads English well enough to comprehend this?"

"Oh, sure. You'd be surprised at how she reads."

Olivia shrugged and picked up another book. Her eyes lit up. "Oh, wonderful! One of my favorite authors. Now I know where I can borrow the new Grafton book."

"Take it now, if you want."

"Oh, no. I'll borrow it when you've finished. Have you read all the other books in the series?"

He squirmed and took a sip from his cup. Damned if he didn't feel sweat pop out. "One or two. It's been a while. He's pretty good. Want another cappuccino?"

She looked at him funny. "I've barely touched this one. Tell me, which of Grafton's is your favorite?"

"I don't recall the title. Like I said, it's been a while. Given any thought to where we might have dinner tonight?"

"Not a bit. But I have given some thought to tomorrow night. You're invited to dinner at my place. I'll even bake a cake for the occasion."

"The occasion?"

She chuckled. "Your birthday. That is, unless you have something else planned."

"Not a thing." He grinned. "Are you really going to bake me a cake?"

"I am. What's your favorite?"

"Coconut."

Olivia must have had rocks in her head. She couldn't believe that she actually promised to make a coconut cake for Jackson. She'd never baked one in her life.

It showed.

One hunk of the top layer started to slide. She

grabbed it and stuck in another half dozen toothpicks to hold it steady. Thank heavens the frosting filled in most of the cracks. She patted it where the cake showed through, then licked the gooey white from her fingers and stepped back.

That wasn't *too* bad. She opened the package of coconut flakes and began to sprinkle them over the sides and top. The top went fine, but there was a logistical problem in getting the coconut to stick to the sides. When she tried tipping the cake, another crevice opened across the top, and she feared for a moment that the whole thing would slide onto the floor. She considered every means that she could think of, including using her blow-dryer to blow it on. In the end, she just slapped on wads of flakes as best she could.

She stepped back and surveyed her work again. It looked worse than a New York street two days after a snowfall.

She sighed. Well, it would have to do. Thank heavens the rest of the meal was simple. She'd shot her budget on pork tenderloin, which was baking in the oven with its plum glaze, as well as Greek salad and roasted new potatoes. She'd bought the Greek salad and new potatoes at the deli. Tessa had given her the recipe for the tenderloin.

The table was set, the candles in place, the gift wrapped and waiting beside his place. She just had time for a quick shower before the birthday boy arrived.

Jackson's head was pounding. He'd taken more aspirin than he thought was sensible, and still his temples throbbed and his eyes ached. He'd tried his damnedest to read that Grafton book last night—and didn't he feel like a fool when he discovered that Grafton was a woman? He'd tried hard, but he just couldn't. He'd finally given up in frustration and stayed up a good part of the night listening to the tape. Thank God the kid at the bookstore had put him on to those tapes. He would have been lost without them.

To top it off, Sunday afternoon was the time that he spent a marathon session with Tami going over all the cases for hearings on Monday morning. He had a legal assistant and another reader at the office, but the worst of it he did with Tami at home. This job, at least all the reading required, was a bitch.

Lord, he hated books. He hated newspapers and magazines and case reports and the backs of cereal boxes. He hated every damned thing in the world that was printed or written or carved in stone—hated it with a passion formed by thirty-odd years of frustration and humiliation and self-disgust. How could he go on pretending to Olivia that what was so wasn't so?

He held his face up to the shower head and turned on the cold water full force, trying to chase away his usual Sunday headache.

Why in the world was he putting himself through such torture? He was a damned fool, that's why.

Then Olivia's face flashed through his mind—her sweet, beautiful, laughing face. No, it was all for Olivia. He'd endure anything for her, do anything to make her happy and see her smile. He didn't know if he could keep up this charade, but he was blamed well going to try.

She was worth it.

She was worth anything he had to do. Thank God for Tami. He wouldn't have a prayer without her. Stephanie was a big help, too. And Jennifer. Maybe he could pay the girls to put in a couple of extra evenings during the week. That might work.

As he sat with Olivia at her little table, Jackson knew for sure that he was the luckiest man alive. She'd served him a fine meal—though he wouldn't have minded a bologna sandwich if they could have shared it. A little bouquet of flowers was in the middle of the table, flanked by candles that she lit before they sat down to eat.

Olivia looked beautiful. Her hair was pinned up, and she wore a kind of loose silky top and pants in fire-engine red that shifted with every move she made, teasing over her curves just enough to drive a man crazy. He had a devil of a time eating that good food. He just wanted to watch her. And touch her. And make love to her until next April. The lady was dynamite.

"That was great," he said, putting down his napkin. "You're a fantastic cook. I'm pleasantly surprised. A beautiful woman who can cook."

She laughed that throaty little laugh that he loved. "Actually I'm not much of a cook, and you'd better withhold judgment until after the cake."

"You really baked me a cake?"

"I really did. It won't win a bake off, but I hope it's edible."

She rose and disappeared into the alcove for a few moments. She returned carrying a white cake with a single tall candle lit in the middle. As she set the plate on the table she smiled and began to sing "Happy Birthday" in a slow, breathless style that reminded him of clips he'd seen of Marilyn Monroe singing to President Kennedy. Damned near drove him wild.

"Happy birthday, Mr.…Commissioner, happy—"

Unable to keep his hands off her another minute, he pulled her down into his lap and kissed away the last words of the song.

She tasted of wine and plum sauce and wildfire. He groaned and probed deeper with his tongue, stroked her breast through the silk and groaned again.

"Lord, I want you," he whispered as he nuzzled her ear.

"But…the cake."

"The cake can wait. Let me make love to you, darlin'."

She tried to say something else, but he kissed away her protests, holding her tight, thrusting his tongue deep. He was about to explode.

"Jackson, no." She pushed him away and struggled to her feet. "I…I don't want this. I'm not ready."

Her cheeks glowed with high color; her chest rose and fell with ragged breaths. She licked her lips.

"Darlin', I'm not much a one to call a lady a liar, but it seems to me that you're about as ready as I am. And let me tell you, I'm *ready*."

Lacing her fingers together tightly, she took a shuddering breath. "I'm sorry. I don't mean to be a tease, but I…it's…it's, uh, a bad time for me."

"Bad—" Then he realized what she was talking about. He nodded. "I see." He unlaced her clamped fingers, which had gone ice-cold, and kissed each hand. "Don't worry about it, sugar. How about that cake?"

She turned and looked at her creation. "It's a mess, isn't it?"

"Darlin', it's the prettiest birthday cake I've ever had—because you made it for me. Let's cut it."

"You have to make a wish and blow out the candle first."

He laughed. "That's a no-brainer." He took a deep breath and blew.

She cut big slabs and handed him a plate. "Careful of the toothpicks. I used nearly a whole box keeping that sucker together. Want some coffee?"

"That would be great. I'll get it." He started to rise, but she motioned him down.

"Stay seated. It's your birthday." She handed him a blue-striped package tied with a bandana bow. "Happy Birthday."

"Oh, honey, you didn't have to get me a present."

"Of course I did. I hope you like it. Open it while I get the coffee."

It looked so pretty that he hated to tear off the paper, but, kid-like, he ripped into it.

A book.

He was holding it in his hands staring at the picture of the kite on the front when she returned with the cups.

Her eyes lit up. "It's a book on the history of kites. Do you like it?"

He swallowed, then smiled. "I love it. What a great present."

She beamed. "I'm glad you like it. How's the cake?"

He carved a bite with his fork, pulled out a couple of toothpicks, then tasted it. "It's damned good."

Looking skeptical, she said, "Are you sure?"

"Positive." And to prove it, he ate two pieces and took the rest of it home with him.

Actually, despite its looks, the cake *was* damned good. He ate another piece before he went to bed. Sitting at the kitchen bar, alone in his big house, he decided that the evening with Olivia had been one of the best birthdays he'd had in recent years. Only one thing could have made it better—to have spent the rest of the night with her.

He wanted her here with him now. He wanted to lay the world at her feet, give her everything her heart desired, make love to her until she moaned with pleasure and said the words he wanted to hear. He wanted—

Patience, he told himself.

Olivia lay in bed thinking. On her back in the darkened room, she stared at shadows made by a sliver of moonlight coming through the blinds.

Why had she chickened out?

She had fully intended for Jackson's birthday party to end here, in this bed. Hadn't she changed the sheets and put sachet under the pillows? Hadn't she worn the most seductive of her lingerie?

The stage was set. He was turned on; she darned sure was. Then, at the last moment—or very near it—

she'd panicked again. The anxiety wasn't as severe as it had been in the park when they'd gone kite flying, but it was there. She thought that she'd reasoned the whole thing through.

Obviously, she hadn't. Why?

She hadn't detected any cruelty or extreme possessiveness in Jackson. He wasn't like Thomas…or her father. He wasn't.

But then Thomas had been wonderful and thoughtful when he was courting her. It was only later that she learned it was all a front, a facade for the controlling, cruel man that he really was. Thomas was a liar of the worst kind. Olivia abhorred lies and deceit. Yet she was finding herself drawn in to doing the very thing she detested.

She hadn't been truthful with Jackson.

But had he been truthful with her?

It was such a small thing, she knew, but why had he claimed to have read Grafton's books when he obviously hadn't? He didn't even know that the famous mystery writer was a woman. She hadn't missed that. And she'd caught him in a couple of other fibs as well.

That's what made her nervous. She was terrified of deception.

No, she couldn't get any more involved with him until she trusted him totally—for Olivia was beginning to realize that she couldn't simply have a no-strings affair with Jackson.

Her heart was at stake.

Jackson had lied about the book. Why?

And what else was he lying about?

Eight

Olivia stood at the sink and watched another of Jackson's "assistants" leave. Heavy caseload, he'd told her. He was having to do a lot of extra work at home. This one was a redhead, tall, gorgeous. Young. Very young. She'd been at Jackson's twice this week. Monday night and Wednesday night.

Not that it was any of her business how many nubile blondes and redheads trooped in and out of his house.

Not that she was jealous.

Liar, liar, pants on fire.

Well, maybe just a tiny bit.

And she realized she was being silly.

She knew that Jackson held a very responsible position in the government and that he took his job seriously. He wasn't messing around with the redhead.

He'd been working. He told her that he planned to work, and she believed him.

But it was odd that none his "assistants" were plump and gray-haired. Or male.

Not her business, she told herself again. She and Jackson weren't a couple; they didn't have any sort of understanding. She had no claim on him.

None.

She quickly turned from the sink, and her gaze fell on the Grafton book that he'd loaned her. She'd just run over and drop it off.

Before she had time to change her mind or scrutinize her motives, Olivia snatched up the book and hurried toward Jackson's house.

It took forever for him to answer the door.

When he finally yanked it open, a green bath sheet draped around his middle and dripping water, he said, "Jennifer, did you for—" Stopping as soon as he spotted Olivia, he grinned and leaned against the jamb. "Well, hello, darlin'. What a pleasant surprise. Come on in."

Mortified, she could only mumble, "Sorry. I...I— Here's your book." She shoved it at him, turned and walked away quickly.

Jackson called after her several times, but she was too embarrassed to stop.

Served her right, she thought. What further evidence did she need? Rumpled sheets? Jackson was a normal, attractive, red-blooded male. Did she think he was celibate? Certainly not. And she had no right to expect it of him.

But if she didn't, why did it hurt so much?

Fighting back tears, she clattered up the stairs to her apartment and hurried inside.

Cursing his fumbling fingers, Jackson zipped his jeans, stomped on his boots and grabbed a T-shirt. He pulled the shirt over his wet head as he strode out of his front door and across the street. What had upset Olivia so? Something sure as hell had, but for the life of him he couldn't figure out what. But then he had a dickens of a headache, and he couldn't think straight. Sticking his head under the cold water usually helped to chase the pain away.

Had he shocked her by coming to the door with a towel around him? Nothing showed. She'd seen him in less when he wore a bathing suit.

Combing his hair with his fingers, he clomped up her stairs. "Olivia!" he shouted, knocking on the glass pane of her door. "Olivia!"

He saw her peek through the curtain as though she didn't know who was banging and caterwauling outside.

The door opened a crack. "Shhhh, you'll wake the dead with all that noise."

He pushed his way inside. "Why did you take off in such an all-fired rush?"

"I...I came at an inopportune time."

"Inopportune how? Because I was in the shower?"

"That and..."

"Spit it out, sugar."

"Well, obviously you and Jennifer—" She glanced away.

"Me and Jennifer...what?"

Olivia stared at the floor.

Then it dawned on him. "You think Jennifer and I—" He laughed. "By damn! You're jealous."

"I am not!"

"You *are!*" He laughed and hugged her to him. "As I live and breathe. You're jealous."

She poked him in the belly with her fist. "I am *not* jealous. I have absolutely no reason to be jealous. What you and Jennifer, or anyone else, do is none of my business."

"Yes, it is, darlin'. I'm not interested in having anyone in my bed but you. And until you're ready, I'll wait. I'm a one-woman man. For the record, Jennifer has a live-in lover who's a wide receiver for the Texas Longhorns. Heck of a nice kid. By the way, want to go to the game Saturday? We can grab some dinner and go boot-scootin' afterward. Ever been boot-scootin'?"

"Nope. I'm not much of a country and western dancer."

"Sugar, you've just never had the right partner. I'm a demon on the dance floor." He grabbed her and did a few fast shuffles and turns.

She laughed. "You're a demon everywhere, Jackson Crow."

He wiggled his eyebrows and winked. "You betcha!"

She pushed away. "How about a cup of coffee?"

"I'd love a cup. Got any aspirins?"

"I think so. Have a headache?"

He rubbed the back of his neck. "Yeah. Too much paperwork."

"Sit down, and I'll get the aspirins."

He didn't have to be told twice. His head was throbbing like a sonofagun.

It must have showed because when she came back, she frowned as she handed him a glass of water and the tablets.

"Do you have these headaches often?"

He shrugged. "Once or twice a week."

"Maybe you need glasses."

He shook his head. "Eyesight's twenty-twenty. It's just a tension headache."

She nodded and stepped behind him. When she started to knead the tight muscles of his neck and shoulders, he couldn't help but moan. "Man, that feels good."

"I used to do this for my father. He had tension headaches."

"You never talk about your family."

"No."

He waited a long time for her to say more. She didn't.

Her magical fingers massaged his scalp, his temples, his forehead, then went back to his neck and shoulders. He felt like he'd died and gone to heaven. The muscles relaxed, the pounding in his head slowly left.

He pulled her down into his lap and touched his forehead to hers, then kissed her gently. "Darlin', I may have to marry you and chain you to my bedpost."

She went stiff as a poker, then sprang to her feet. "In your dreams, Commissioner."

Damn! He'd set her off again. When was he ever going to learn not to crowd Olivia? He'd finally wormed enough out of Irish to know that her ex had been a serious control freak, and her daddy was, too. At the first sight of a rein, Olivia would bolt and run. Patience was the key. Patience to let her set the pace.

That ex-husband of hers must have been a real scumbag. Somebody ought to do him some serious damage for screwing up Olivia's life so badly.

Olivia hadn't been to a football game in…well, she couldn't even remember the last one. Certainly not since she'd been in college, she thought as she'd dressed in slacks, two-piece blue sweater set and loafers. She hoped she looked okay.

She needn't have worried. They'd sat with a gang of Jackson's old buddies and their ladies in the special club section of the stadium reserved for those who were big contributors to the school. Part of the group wore yuppie casual chic and part wore Western garb similar to Jackson's, though she had to admit that his jeans, plaid shirt and black felt hat looked twice as good on him. Everybody had yelled for the Texas Longhorns, laughed and eaten peanuts and popcorn and hot dogs.

Jennifer's boyfriend made two touchdowns, and they won twenty-seven to ten. Olivia had a terrific time.

"Are you a University of Texas alum?" she asked Jackson as they exited through the clubroom.

He grinned. "Sort of. I flunked out my first year. But I made a lot of friends. It's the best party school in the state. I always make a hefty donation so I can have good seats and decent parking at the football games."

"Jackson! That's terrible."

"It's the truth. Want me to lie about it?"

She shook her head and smiled. "No, of course not." That was Jackson. He was a straight shooter. That was one of the things she found endearing about him.

They went to their favorite Mexican restaurant, though Olivia was hard-pressed to find room for food after the junk she'd consumed at the game. She settled on a salad, and they ate on the patio. Although Olivia had experienced only a few cool nights since her move to Austin, she was amazed that the weather was still balmy enough in November to sit outside. Any chill was chased away with fragrant mesquite wood burning in a clay firepot.

After their leisurely meal, they went to a big barn-looking building and parked. Jackson's pickup truck fitted right in with the sea of others parked out front. She could already feel and hear the twang and rumble of the bass inside.

As she stepped down from the cab, a dozen "yee-haws" split the air, and the sound of a fiddle plucked strings of excitement inside her. By the time they went inside she was quivering on the inside and laughing on the outside, wiggling her shoulders and bobbling her head to the infectious beat.

Jackson slipped a bill to the waiter, and he led them to a table near the dance floor, where couples in a wild mixture of hats and jeans and designer capris whirled and stomped around the floor. Neon sizzled in reds, blues, yellows and greens, and beer flowed from endless pitchers and long-necked bottles. The music's potent throb vibrated the floor beneath their feet and challenged all comers to join in the revelry.

Jackson didn't even let her sit down. "Yee-hawww! Sugar, let's boogie."

He pulled her onto the floor with him, and, with a loose-hipped rhythm, swung her around and strutted with the counter-clockwise flow of the dancers. How she followed him, she didn't know—maybe it was a result of Miss Melear's dance classes—but follow him she did.

"Darlin', you're a natural," he said, grinning as he pushed and twirled and two-stepped to the loud country band.

They danced for a half hour solid until the band took a break. Decidedly damp from the exertion, Olivia fanned her face with her fingers, then mopped it with the handkerchief Jackson offered.

She plunked down in her chair and took a big swig of the bottled water she'd ordered earlier. "I'm not sure my heart can take this," she said. "I'm exhausted."

He laughed. "You're doing great. I thought you said you'd never done any country and western dancing."

"I haven't, but it's not too hard—especially if you've had twelve years of dance lessons and watched country music programs on TV. Plus, you're darned good and have a strong lead."

"Thank you, ma'am. What kind of dance lessons did you have in...?"

"California," she supplied, being vague about her origins as usual. "Tap, ballet, jazz, ballroom. My mother insisted—I think because she always wanted to take dancing when she was a child. Then after my mother...died, my father insisted that I keep it up. He contended that it encouraged discipline."

"Did it?"

"I suppose. Mostly it kept me busy and out of his hair."

Jackson took a swallow from his long-neck, then asked, "How old were you when your mother died?"

"Ten. She...she took an overdose of sleeping pills. I found her when I came home from school."

"Oh, darlin'," he said laying his hand over hers. "I'm sorry."

"It was a long time ago. And I don't want to think about it tonight. I'm having too much fun. Want to play some pool?" She nodded in the direction of the tables filling an anteroom.

He cocked one dark eyebrow. "*You* play pool?"

"What's so strange about that? Bet I can beat you."

"Bite your tongue, sugar. I have a degree in pool."

She grinned. "I thought it was poker."

"Double major. Put your money where your mouth is."

"Five dollars," she said.

"You're on."

She, to borrow one of Jackson's colorful phrases, cleaned his plow. Cleared the table her first time up.

One hand on his hip, Jackson leaned on his cue and watched her. When the last ball dropped, he shook his head. "I think I've just been hustled."

Olivia laughed. "I told you I was good."

"Where'd you learn?"

"From my brother. When he got in trouble, my

father would ground him, and he would head for the third-floor billiard room. I felt sorry for Jason, so I'd tag along to keep him company. He was in trouble a lot."

"I've never heard you mention your brother before."

"No."

"You see much of him?"

She shook her head. "I don't even know where he is. Jason left home the day he turned eighteen. I haven't seen him since. Say," she said, changing the subject before she got maudlin—or revealed more than she wanted to, "the band's back. I want to learn to line dance."

"Let's do it."

Olivia soon caught on to the steps and was keeping up with the most experienced of the crowd. Afterward Jackson taught her several other dances, but it was the slow ones that he liked best.

"I get to hold you close," he said, shooting her a wicked grin, then pulling her into his arms.

She had to admit that she liked the slow dances, too. With her forehead on his cheek, the top of her head fitted perfectly under his hat brim. Instead of taking the usual hand and arm position, he put both arms around her waist—after tucking hers around him.

After a couple of turns around the floor, slipping her fingers into the back pockets of his jeans seemed a very good idea.

Excellent, in fact. And rather cheeky. She almost laughed allowed at her Freudian slip. In fact, Freud would have had a field day with her stream of consciousness at that moment.

She'd never realized how erotic a man's posterior could be. Well…not just any man's. Jackson's.

His butt turned her on like crazy.

Taut, sinewy, sexy. His muscles moved and rippled slowly under her fingers.

He pulled her closer against him, and she realized that he was turned on as well. She tried to pull away, but he held her tight.

"But, you're getting, uh, er…"

"Hard as a rock," he supplied. "Yes, ma'am. But I'll survive. The man who made a cowboy's jeans tight was one smart hombre."

It was after midnight when they finally decided to call it a night. The honky-tonk was still rocking, but Olivia was pooped.

Outside, Jackson put his arm around her as they walked to the truck. "Have a good time?" he asked.

"Wonderful." She snuggled into the crook of his arm. The wind had kicked up, and the temperature had dropped considerably. "It's cold." She shivered against him.

"Front moving in."

The sky flashed with a streak of lightning, and a couple of seconds later thunder rolled through the hills. A few fat drops of rain pelted them.

Jackson plunked his black cowboy hat on her head. "Let's make a run for it before the bottom falls out."

They almost made it.

Yards before they reached the truck, the sky opened and a torrent of cold rain drenched them.

Jackson tried to shield her, but it was no use, they were both soaked and shivering by the time they made it inside the cab. He started the truck and pulled away, the wipers sluicing on high.

"It'll take a minute for the heater to get warm," he told her.

"How did it get so cold so quickly?" she asked, her teeth chattering.

"Texas weather."

She tried to dry off with a handful of paper napkins Jackson found under his seat. It was a futile effort. The only place on her that was dry was under the hat she still wore.

He turned the heater on. After an initial blast of cold air, blessed warmth began to push away some of the chill. Jackson leaned forward, concentrating on seeing the road through the deluge, and she watched him concentrate.

Never in her life had just looking at a man thrilled her so, set her blood to boiling and robbed her of sanity. All she could think about was taking off that wet shirt he wore and licking the raindrops from his chest and his face. She ached to feel his hands on her bare skin.

She squirmed in the leather seat, and he glanced at her. His thoughts must have been following the same line as hers. Raw desire etched his face, and he reached over and stroked her thigh.

His touch sent a shiver of electricity zinging through her; she sucked in a startled breath. Only the restraint of her seat belt kept her from doing something foolish. Sexual awareness bombarded the cab, ricocheted off the walls in frenzied currents, scorched the air.

He moved his hand from her leg, seized the wheel in a two-handed grip, and said, "I gotta pay attention to what I'm doing. I sure as hell don't want to wreck us now."

"No. Not now." Was that her voice? It sounded raspy, breathless.

Jackson drove safely, but quickly, to their neighborhood. He didn't pull into her drive; he headed straight for his own, poking the remote to lift the garage door as he made the turn.

She made a sound of protest and looked toward her apartment.

"We'd get soaked again going to your place," he said as he pulled into the garage. "Besides, my bed is bigger." He grinned. "And I'm gonna need a *lot* of room."

Nine

"Come on in," Jackson said, "and let's get you dry and warmed up. You're soaked to the skin."

"You're just as wet as I am."

"Yeah, but I'm tough."

She poked his arm as he guided her through the mudroom door. "I'm tough, too."

He kissed her nose. "No, you're like spun sugar, and I can't have you melting on me."

Streak, who had been left in the room with his basket and newspapers, started barking and jumping on Jackson.

"Hey, there, fella," he said, bending to scratch the puppy's head. "How's the food and water holding out? Looks good. You stay here and guard the house, and I'm going to take care of the lady."

As if he'd understood every word, Streak barked

and wiggled his tail. Jackson could charm anybody—woman or beast.

He led her through the kitchen, where they pulled off shoes and boots, to the den. "Let me get a fire going. You go to the guest bath and get out of those wet clothes. Down the hall, second door on the right. There should be an extra robe in the linen closet."

Olivia didn't argue. She was soaking and chilled to the bone.

The guest bath, beautifully decorated in dusky green and terra-cotta, still smelled of newness. As she unbuttoned her sweater, she caught her reflection in the mirror and realized that not only did she look totally bedraggled, but she still wore Jackson's black cowboy hat. She took it off and set it on the tile counter, then stripped off her wet clothes and draped them over the shower rod.

After toweling off, she found a stack of white terry robes in the closet and took one. Crow's Nest was embroidered in black on the breast pocket. It was too big, but she belted it snugly, then searched the drawers hoping to find a hair-dryer and a brush. She did. Clever decorator, she supposed. Everything for the guest's comfort. She even found an unopened box of condoms in one of the drawers.

She opened them. Feeling a bit wicked, she put one packet in the pocket of her robe and gave it a pat.

Using the dryer she'd found, she fluffed the damp ends of her hair and restored a bit of order, then leaned forward toward the large mirror and checked for mascara smudges. Her reflection told her that she looked decidedly mussed. The shivery rasp of terry cloth across her nipples told her that she felt decidedly sensual. The gleam in her eyes told her that she was decidedly ready for Jackson Crow.

This was it. This was the night.

Feeling even more wicked, she put two more packets in her robe pocket and smiled as she picked up his hat and left the bathroom.

Barefoot, she walked back to the den. She stopped at the doorway. Jackson was squatted in front of the fireplace, adding another log to the new fire. He was barefoot, too.

And bare-chested.

Olivia's breath caught as she watched him poke the log. A shower of sparks shot upward, the cozy scent of burning oak pervaded the room and the glow of the flames brushed his skin with copper. He wore only an oft-washed pair of jeans, and a towel lay draped around his neck. His dark hair was rumpled and waving as if he'd merely scrubbed the towel over his head a couple of times.

He must have sensed her presence, or perhaps she'd made some small sound, for he glanced at her over his shoulder and smiled. He stood and held out his hand. "Fire's going pretty good. Come warm yourself. I've got coffee brewing—or would you rather have wine?"

"Coffee first."

She joined him. "Nice fire."

"Naturally. I was a Boy Scout."

"I'll bet you were cute in your uniform."

"Absolutely."

"Here's your hat."

"It looks better on you." He plunked it on her head, then pulled her into his arms and kissed her.

His lips were still cool from the outside chill, but his tongue was warm. Hot.

And reckless.

He pulled her closer, and the hat tumbled from her head as she arched her body against him.

He kissed her thoroughly, then left her mouth to nuzzle his way down to her shoulder, pushing aside the robe as he went. She clung to his bare back as his lips traced her collarbone, sighed as he rubbed his cheek against the cap of her shoulder, groaned as his hands slipped inside her robe to cup her bottom.

"Oh, darlin'," he moaned against her ear as he stroked her breast, and she turned into pudding.

She ached for him, ached with a need so potent that she could hardly stand it. She'd wanted him for a long time, and to wait any longer was excruciating. Grinding herself against him, she grabbed handfuls of his hair and pulled his mouth to hers. Her breath was ragged; her heart pounded furiously.

"Oh, Jackson, I want—I want—"

"What do you want, darlin'?"

"I want you."

"You've got me."

He kissed her again, rubbing his chest across her breasts, pushing the robe farther and farther apart until it was skin against skin. His hand stole between them to thumb her nipple, then it dipped lower, and her knees went weak.

"Jackson," she whimpered.

"What, darlin'?"

"I want—I want—"

"Tell me what you want, sugar."

His fingers were doing marvelous things to her. She

could barely find words. "I want you. Inside me. Now."

He eased her down to the couch, and her robe fell open.

He knelt beside her, his eyes seeming to devour her. "In a minute, darlin'. I've got some more looking to do. And some more touching." He dipped his tongue into her navel. "I want to make sure you're ready."

His hand stroked up her thigh, over her belly, and up to make a figure eight across her breasts, then down again to probe more intimate places.

"Jackson, I'm ready!"

He chuckled. "I believe you are. I'll be right back."

He stood.

"Where are you *going?*"

"To get some protection."

She fished in the robe pocket. "Here."

He cocked one wicked dark brow and grinned. "Prepared were we?"

"I told you I was ready."

"So you did, sugar. I was beginning to think it wasn't going to happen." He stripped off his jeans, then kissed her while he put on the protection. "I've lain awake many a night imagining this moment."

He continued to stroke her and kiss her as he moved to a place between her thighs. She sucked in a long gasp as he slid into her, filling her deeply, completely.

They savored the moment of their joining, lying still for several seconds. A rush of wonderment swept over her, and she drank in the power of their coupling.

Then they began to move as one in a slow sensual dance that stoked sparks of desire in every cell of her body.

He stroked her as they moved, whispered praise for her body, her beauty as he thrust deeper and deeper. She rose to meet each thrust, and the power and tempo increased until the flames glowed white-hot.

Their lovemaking grew frenzied, and she bucked and groaned, and they rolled off the couch onto the rug.

Hotter and hotter, faster and faster—

Then spasms broke over her. They arched her back and stole her breath.

His climax came almost immediately.

She could feel the throb of his fulfillment. His back bowed and his arms taut, holding his weight off her, and with firelight glistening off his damp skin, he looked like a great primitive warrior. Strong, muscled, virile, supremely handsome.

Her heart ached at the sight.

Dear Lord, how she loved him.

Loved?

No, she told herself. She'd loved the lovemaking. He was a skilled lover. He'd made her feel like the only woman in the world for him.

She would bask in the feelings for now, enjoy the temporary intimacy.

Olivia crossed her arms behind his neck, pulled him down to her and snuggled close.

"Sugar, I do believe you're purring."

She chuckled and, imitating his drawl, said, "Sugar, I do believe you're right. That was delicious."

"The night is young yet, tiger. Want some coffee? Some wine? Some cheese? My heart on a pine plank?"

"You're crazy."

"Yes, ma'am. Crazy about you."

The storm continued throughout the night, and their tempestuous coupling continued, as well. They moved to Jackson's big bed, snuggling and napping, then rousing to make love again, both insatiable, wild. Was it the thunder and lightning, vibrating through the house and splitting the sky with its power, that roused her to such wildness, such abandon? Or was it simply Jackson? Never had a man stirred her the way Jackson did. Never had a man satisfied her the way Jackson did.

She slept, content and secure, in his arms.

Shortly before dawn Olivia woke. The storm had moved on, and the rain had stopped. She slipped from his bed and went to the guest bathroom. Her clothes were still damp. She hesitated to put on the clammy garments, but she didn't want to be seen skittering across the street in a robe, either.

Deciding to put her things through the dryer, she slipped on a robe and gathered up her belongings, then moved quietly to the laundry area off the mudroom.

As soon as she opened the door, Streak met her with excited barks and wiggles and jumps.

"Shhhh," she said, closing the door behind her. "We don't want to wake up your master. He had a very tiring night."

Streak wasn't very concerned about being quiet. He

barked and wiggled and jumped until she dumped her clothes in the dryer and picked him up.

"You rascal."

He licked her nose. She laughed.

"Hey, buddy," Jackson said from the doorway. "Are you trying to smooch my gal?"

Startled by his presence, Olivia turned. "Did we wake you? I'm sorry. I told Streak to be quiet, but he doesn't mind very well."

"You got that right. But the noise didn't wake me. The quiet did. I missed the sound of your breathing. What are you doing up so early?"

"Drying my clothes. I didn't want to sneak home wearing your robe and be the talk of the neighborhood."

"Don't worry about it. Come on back to bed and get some sleep."

She gave him a teasing smile. "I'm afraid that if I go back to bed with you, I won't get any sleep."

A wicked grin broke over his face. "You're safe for a while, darlin'. I'm plumb tuckered out. Come on." He held out his hand.

She took it and followed him back to his big bed.

He lied. Or else he got his second wind.

It was midmorning before she awoke. Alone.

Just as she sat up and stretched, Jackson stuck his head in the room. "Mornin', sugar. How do you like your eggs?"

"Poached."

"Will scrambled do?"

She smiled. "Sure."

"Good. I'll be right back."

In two minutes he came back, carrying a tray. He wore only his jeans.

"Breakfast in bed?" she asked.

"Yep. Eggs, bacon, biscuits, butter, jelly, orange juice and coffee. The jelly is homemade. Grandpa Pete puts up several pints every year when the dewberries come in." He put the bed tray over her lap, then slathered butter and jelly on a piece of biscuit and held it to her mouth.

She took the bit he offered. "Mmm. Very good. Where's your breakfast?"

"I already ate mine. And yours. Twice. Streak helped some."

Frowning, she tried to figure out what he'd just said.

He laughed. "I fixed breakfast earlier, but you went back to sleep. So I went ahead and ate. I thought you might be rousing about an hour ago, so I fixed you another breakfast. You were sawing logs when I brought it." He grinned. "I figured that the third time was a charm. Need anything else?"

Touched by his thoughtfulness, she swallowed back the lump in her throat and shook her head. "Thank you very much. Nobody ever brought me breakfast in bed before."

"Not even when you were sick or on your birthday?"

She shook her head again. "Not that I recall. Thank you, Jackson. Thank you very much."

"No problem." He gave her a peck and crawled in beside her. "Want to watch the news?" He picked up the TV remote control and clicked it on.

"Fine with me. Have you read the Sunday paper already?" She sipped her coffee.

"I don't take a newspaper."

"Good heavens, why not? I can't start the day without coffee and the morning paper. Sundays are a special treat. On Sundays, I take both the *Statesman* and the *New York Times.*"

"Never liked to take the time for newspapers. Guess I'm a TV kind of guy. Want me to go get the papers from your driveway?"

"No, I'll read them later. I can't believe that you don't subscribe to a newspaper, especially now that you're in politics," she said in a teasing way. "I mean, how can you keep up with Doonesbury?"

"Is that such a loss? Look, I've got instant news around the world with CNN—and I can shave at the same time."

Olivia rolled her eyes and buttered another bite of biscuit. "Jackson, that's ludicrous. You can't get the depth of information from a TV show that you can get from a newspaper. TV is just a series of sound bytes. Newspapers give details."

"I listen to the radio for the details."

She sighed. "Deliver me."

He chuckled and took a bite of the biscuit she held. "To any place in particular?" He dabbed a bit of jelly on her chin and licked it off.

He tugged down the sheet that was tucked under her arms and put another dab on her nipple. "Have I told you how much I love your breasts?" He bent and licked the jelly smear away, lingering to lick long after the sweetness had disappeared.

"Mmmmmm. Several times. Careful, you're jostling the coffee."

He moved the tray from her lap to the floor.

"What about my breakfast?"

"I'll fix you another later." He ripped the sheet away.

Jackson wondered later why he hadn't told her. He'd had the perfect opening while she was eating breakfast and they were talking about newspapers. Why hadn't he told her the truth? Why hadn't he just told her that he hated the sight of newspapers along with everything else that was printed?

Why hadn't he just spilled his guts and told her what a damned moron he was? He felt like a dirty dog by not telling her the truth. He wanted things to be open and aboveboard between them. But he wanted her respect more. If she knew, how could somebody like her respect somebody like him?

He broke out in a cold sweat when he thought of her knowing his secret. She was so sharp, a damned brilliant woman. A scholar. He couldn't abide the notion of Olivia pitying him or being embarrassed by his ignorance.

Sooner or later, she was bound to find out.

Maybe not. Maybe he could keep faking it. After all, he was an expert at faking it. He'd faked it all the way through school and through all his adult life.

Hell, even his own family didn't suspect that he could barely read.

Ten

Late the following Sunday afternoon, Olivia hummed as she iced a coconut cake. She couldn't believe that she was feeling so domestic. After the disastrous birthday production, she'd sworn off cake making. Yet, she and Jackson had only been lovers a week and already she was baking again. She must be fond of the guy.

She smiled and stepped back and surveyed her latest effort. Not bad.

In fact, it looked darned good.

She picked it up and took it downstairs, calling to Tessa and Ed as she spotted them in the backyard. She and Jackson were joining Tessa and Ed for barbecue. Jackson was providing the beer; Olivia, the dessert.

Ed, a tall, silver-haired man, waved his mop brush

at her. "Do you smell those ribs? My mouth's already watering."

"They smell great. Are they almost done?" Olivia asked as she set the cake on a picnic table near Tessa.

"Another half hour ought to do it."

"Nice cake," Tessa said.

Olivia beamed proudly at the compliment. "There's something to be said for practice."

"I'll take it inside," Tessa said. "It's getting a bit cool to eat outdoors, don't you think?"

"Aw, you gals are sissies," Ed said. "It's pleasant out here. Say, where's Jackson with the beer?"

"He should be here," Olivia said. "I told him five-thirty."

Glancing across the street, she saw that Tami's car was gone. In fact, she recalled that Tami had left the usual Sunday-afternoon session quite a bit earlier than she ordinarily did.

Odd that Jackson hadn't arrived. He was always punctual.

"I'll run over and see what's keeping him," she told the Jurneys.

She hurried across the street and through the courtyard. After ringing the bell twice and receiving no answer, she grew concerned and tried the door. It was unlocked. She went inside, stopped and called out.

Nothing.

She searched the den and the kitchen. Then, thinking that he might have gone out for a quick errand, she checked the garage. Both his pickup and his Jaguar were in their places. Retracing her steps, she had started down the hallway to his bedroom when she heard a loud crash and muffled cursing coming from Jackson's study.

She hurried to the door and knocked. "Jackson!"

She knocked again, then opened the door. Only a dim desk lamp illuminated the room.

"Dammit!" Jackson shouted, hurling a sheaf of pages against a wall and letting out a string of vitriolic oaths.

Papers flew everywhere, and Olivia gasped at his behavior. "Jackson! What on earth is wrong?"

He turned to her, anguish, soul-deep and terrible, etching his face, despair burning from his eyes. He raked his fingers through his hair, then clamped them against his skull as if holding his head on. "I can't do it, Olivia. I can't. Dammit, I'm such a loser. You deserve better than me."

He slumped to his chair, put his elbows on his desk and dropped his forehead into his hands.

Alarmed by a Jackson she'd never seen before, a thousand thoughts went through her mind. Was he drunk? On drugs? Psychotic? She'd never seen him in a fit of temper, and it frightened her. Witnessing his behavior brought a torrent of old memories rushing into her head, memories that carried heavy emotions with them.

Her impulse was to hasten to Jackson's side and comfort his obvious pain.

She hesitated, shuddering as tapes of her father and of Thomas flashed through her mind, the countless times she'd suffered through their vehement outbursts, been left battered and demoralized. The sequence was always the same. First came their rage and violence, then contrition, often sorrowful self-abasement and empty promises. She'd endured enough of such behavior to last a dozen lifetimes.

Was Jackson the same sort of man?

No, she prayed. *Please, God, no. Not Jackson.*

She couldn't believe that she'd ended up repeating her mistakes, falling into the same pattern. Women did it all the time, ended up choosing a clone of fathers or former partners.

No. She wouldn't believe it. Jackson was a different cut of man, and she was a different woman from the one she'd been when she was younger. She was wiser, more experienced.

Wasn't she?

Dear Lord, she hoped so.

Her hesitation lasted only a moment more before she went to him, knelt beside his chair and laid her hand on his thigh.

"Jackson, what's wrong?"

Seconds seemed like hours.

Finally Jackson lifted his head. His expression was no less anguished. "I'm a stupid son-of-a-bitch. Damned stupid. And a fake. I'm a fake."

"Jackson, what are you talking about? I don't understand. Why are you so angry? What's going on?"

"Oh, hell, this is a mess." He swiped his hands over his face, then dropped his head back and stared at the ceiling. "Tami's little boy got sick, and she had to go home, and I can't locate Jennifer or any of the others that usually help. Hell, nobody's home on Sunday afternoon. I've got this whole blasted bunch of cases to go over before the hearings tomorrow, and I can't do it. I've been sitting here for two damned hours trying. Wanna know how far I've gotten? Two pages. Two measly, sorry-assed pages. A page an hour.'' He gave a hollow bark of laughter and rubbed his forehead. ''I'm about as sharp as a rubber knife.''

''One of those headaches?''

''It feels like somebody's hammering roofing nails into my skull.''

''I'm sorry. Where are the aspirins?''

''Right here.'' He jerked out the drawer and dropped the bottle onto the desk top. ''Aspirins won't help. I've already taken a handful.''

She stood. ''Then one of my massages ought to do the trick.'' Her fingers went to his shoulders, but he caught her hands and pulled her into his lap.

He cradled her close and laid his cheek on her head. ''Darlin', I'd sooner fight the devil with a willow switch than admit this to you, but I've gotta do it. I've been wrestling with it for a while now, and if anything is to become of us, there's no way around it. I've got to tell you the truth about me.''

He took a deep shuddering breath, and panic began to build inside Olivia. What was he trying to say? Her imagination raced from one wild notion to another. Did he have a secret wife? A terrible communicable disease? Some shocking sexual perversion?

''Is it...bad?'' she asked.

''Bad enough.''

One part of her wanted to clamp her hands over her ears or over his mouth to hold back this awful thing that he was about to reveal. The more sensible part of her said quietly, ''What truth?''

She could hear his watch tick.

''I can't read.''

The tension left her muscles, and Olivia laughed.

"Of course you can't read. You have a splitting headache." She pulled him to her and kissed his forehead. "Poor baby."

He captured her hands, kissed first one palm, then the other, then looked earnestly into her eyes. "Listen to me, love. I...can't...read. Headache or no. I...can't...read."

Puzzled, she stared at him. "Are you trying to tell me that you're *illiterate?*"

"All but."

She sat up straight. "That's ridiculous. You have a college degree. How can you be illiterate?"

"I didn't say I wasn't resourceful. I flunked out of four schools—some sooner than others—before I landed in the one where I got my degree. It's an...unusual college, small and unaccredited, kind of...experimental. I got my degree in dramatic arts."

"Dramatic arts? As in acting?"

"Well, yeah. I wasn't too bad at it. I'd always been a ham and the class clown."

"To hide the fact that you couldn't read."

He shrugged. "Maybe. I've never tried to analyze it."

"Your parents don't know?"

"Nope. I was always ashamed of how stupid I was compared to everybody else in the family."

"Jackson, I've known you for quite a while, and I'm very sure that you're not stupid. In fact, Pete told me that you're the smartest of his grandchildren."

"Me?"

"Yes, you. Didn't your elementary school teachers ever catch on that you were having problems?"

"Not really. Oh, I learned to read some, that is, I

could recognize words on flash cards, but developing a phenomenal memory got me by.'' He chuckled, but there was no mirth in the sound. ''I used the cookies from my lunch box to bribe a couple of kids in my class. They'd read the lesson to me, and I'd memorize it. If we had to read aloud, I'd always volunteer to be first so I'd know where to start, things like that. As I said, I learned to be resourceful. I was never much of a student, but I managed.''

''You compensated.'' She hugged him close, thinking of the little boy struggling with his awful secret.

''Yeah, I suppose. But this time I got in over my head. All the reading that goes along with being a railroad commissioner is a bitch.''

''That's what Tami and Jennifer and the other girls do,'' Olivia said. ''They read for you.''

''Yeah. They think I have an eye problem. Like I said, I'm resourceful when it comes to hiding my ignorance.''

''Have you actually had your vision tested?''

He nodded. ''It really is twenty-twenty. And through the years, I've hired tutors on the sly a time or two, trying to learn to read, but it's no use. The letters start running together, and they might as well be chicken tracks dancing around on the page. God, I hate telling you this. It's humiliating.'' He stared at the ceiling some more.

''Don't be silly. I'm a psychologist—or soon will be, anyway. I suspect that you have some specific learning difficulty—a form of dyslexia would be my first guess. We won't know exactly until we have you tested.''

''Tested? What's dyslexia?''

"Yes, tested. And I'm not an expert in the field, but, basically, the wiring in some people's brains is different, and signals get scrambled so that reading is difficult. Dyslexia is a wastebasket term that covers a range of perceptual problems."

"Great. Now I'm a freak with a miswired brain. I'm not sure that it wasn't better just to be dumb."

Olivia bit back a smile. "You aren't a freak. Or dumb. Lots of people are dyslexic—would you believe Albert Einstein, Thomas Edison and Pablo Picasso among others? And there are many kinds of dyslexia." She stood and walked to the wall switch. "Let me get some proper light in here, and I'll show you."

Jackson winced at the brightness. "Actually, I do better with dimmer light."

"Hmm," Olivia said as a thought suddenly struck her. Headaches, words moving on the page, now photosensitivity. "Does strong light bother you? Is that why you wear your sunglasses so much?"

"I suppose. But everybody wears sunglasses."

"That may be a clue, but I'll have to talk to JoAnna."

"Who's JoAnna?"

"She's a friend of mine from the university. She's doing her doctoral research on a special kind of reading difficulty and some new and unconventional techniques for ameliorating the problem. JoAnna's a whiz at this kind of stuff. We'll set up an appointment for her to test you."

He looked uncomfortable, and she chuckled. "It's painless. I promise. And speaking of pain, how's your headache?"

"Better. Almost gone. I guess confession is good for the head as well as the soul. But I still feel like a dope."

"Why? I told you that lots of very bright people have similar problems. And at least it's not catching. I was afraid that you were going to tell me that you had some dread disease."

He grinned. "Nope. I'm clean."

"Good. Tell you what. Let's go pig out on Ed's barbecued ribs, and then we'll come back here, and I'll read whatever you need to bone up on for tomorrow."

He stood and tucked in his shirt. "You're on. I could eat a dozen of those ribs right now."

"Then let's get the beer and go."

They walked to the kitchen where Jackson retrieved two six-packs from the fridge and set them on the counter. He took her into his arms and kissed her—a long, slow, sweet kiss.

"Have I told you what a very special lady you are?" he asked. "You never cease to amaze me."

"I never think of myself as amazing."

"You are. I sweated blood over telling you about—you know—and you didn't even bat an eyelash."

"Why would I? Your problem isn't shameful. We can handle it."

He smiled at her, and an expression of infinite tenderness came over his face. "You're something else."

He kissed her again, almost reverently. "We'd better get a move on."

"You're right. We don't want to miss out on the

ribs. And I baked a coconut cake. Without a single crack.''

He laughed and grabbed the beer.

''Where's Streak?''

''Oops. I forgot about the little dickens. He was banished to the patio for chewing up one of my favorite golfing boots.''

''Golfing boots? You play golf in *boots?*''

''Yep. I have a pair of boots for just about everything.'' He held up one foot and showed off a pair of well-worn black ones. ''Now, these are my eating ribs and drinking beer boots.'' He grinned.

''Oh, you!'' She laughed and swatted his bottom.

''Miss Olivia! Such liberties.'' He gave her a quick peck. ''Let me tend to the animal, and we'll go.''

After Streak was fed, watered and left in the mud room with newspapers, they went out the front door.

Outside, dark was falling, and as they crossed the street, they could see Tessa and Ed waiting on the porch. ''Darlin','' Jackson said quietly, ''if you don't mind, I'd just as soon you didn't mention my, uh, problem to the Jurneys.''

''My lips are sealed. I won't tell a soul but JoAnna.''

On Tuesday afternoon Jackson felt like a wiggletail in hot ashes as he paced the hall waiting for Olivia's class to be over. His boots were too tight and his tie choked him and he thought he might be coming down with a fever.

He jiggled the change in his pocket and paced some more.

Finally the door opened and a deluge of students

poured through the door. Was he getting old or were college kids getting younger? And he couldn't believe the garb they wore to class.

When the herd cleared, he stepped inside the room. Olivia was at the lectern talking to several lingering class members. As he approached, one of the girls elbowed another standing beside her. They stared at him, looked at each other, then giggled.

Yep, he must be getting old.

In a few minutes the stragglers left, and the two gigglers giggled again as they passed him.

Olivia grinned as he approached. "You really are a hottie."

"A *hottie?*"

"That's a compliment. Bridget and Emily think that you're very handsome."

"Who are Bridget and Emily?"

"The gigglers."

He grinned. "A hottie, huh?"

"Don't let it go to your head, Commissioner. If you were precocious, you could be their father."

"Don't rub it in. I feel 103 today. Is the meeting with JoAnna still on?"

Olivia nodded and glanced at her watch. "She should be in the lab by now. Nervous?"

"Naw. I always trim my fingernails with my teeth."

She laughed and tucked her arm through the crook of his elbow. "Come on. I'll introduce you to JoAnna. And, by the way, you really do look very handsome today."

He glanced down at his gray suit. "These are my

commissioner duds. I came straight from the office. Are you going to stay with me while I get tested?''

''Do you want me to?''

''I don't know. One part of me says yes, I want you glued to my side. Another part doesn't want you to witness my humiliation.''

''Why don't we ask JoAnna what she thinks?''

They went to a room on the next floor, and Olivia introduced him to a short woman with a bush of kinky red hair. She had a friendly smile and a handshake like a linebacker. They shot the breeze for a few minutes, then JoAnna Armbruster suggested that Olivia drop back by in a couple of hours.

''I hate for you to hang around so long waiting for me,'' he told Olivia. ''Why don't you go on home, and I'll stop by later.''

''Sure?''

''Positive.'' He winked. ''Thanks.''

''Take off your coat and relax,'' JoAnna told him after Olivia left. ''I promise this will be painless. Want a glass of water?''

''Please.'' He stripped off his coat and tie and rolled up his sleeves, then downed the glass of water in one gulp.

''Nervous?''

''Does it show?''

She gave a laugh that seemed twice her size and motioned him to a chair. First she asked a lot of questions and filled out a form, then she had him read a bunch of stuff and asked him some more questions. That went on for a while, and his head began to pound.

After more questions and some *hmms* she opened

a folder and removed several colored plastic sheets. "I think that Olivia was right. I think that you may have Scotopic Sensitivity Syndrome, also known as Irlen Syndrome."

"Say what? Is it catching?"

She laughed. "Not the last I heard, but if I'm right, you'll make a dynamite subject for my study. Irlen Syndrome is a perceptual problem named after Helen Irlen, the woman who first diagnosed it. Read this for me." She pointed to one of the pages on the desk.

He labored with the words as the letters danced and converged.

"Okay, try this." She laid two sheets of colored plastic over the page.

It wasn't any better.

After trying several combinations, she laid a purple and a turquoise sheet over the page. "Now try."

Growing more disheartened by the moment, he sighed and looked at the page.

He glanced up at JoAnna, then looked at the page again. "Well, I'll be damned."

"What?"

"The letters. They're not moving. They're not dancing or blurring or sliding off the page. They're just sitting there—as clear as can be. Well, I'll be damned."

A grin broke over his face, and he let out a whoop.

The grin stayed on his face while they finished the session and JoAnna put the specific colored overlays into an envelope for him.

"Placing these over the pages will help you read books or other printed material," she told him, "but you should also be fitted for special filtered lenses at a clinic. The glasses are expensive, but I think you'll be amazed at how much they will help you." She handed him a sheet of paper. "This is a list of locations in the United States that do testing for filters."

"JoAnna, I can't tell you what this means to me." He cleared his throat. Twice. Damn! For a little of nothing, he would start bawling like a baby. "It's a miracle."

She smiled. "The difference is so dramatic with some people that I know it seems that way sometimes. You're one of the lucky ones."

"You don't have to tell me twice. Listen, do you need any help with your studies? A grant or something?"

"Are you kidding? Grad students always need grants."

He whipped out his checkbook, wrote a sizable check and handed it to her.

Her eyes widened when she saw the amount. "You've made a mistake. I—I can't take this. This is for—"

"It's for a drop in the bucket compared to what you've done for me. Take it." He pumped her hand again and strode from the room.

Olivia sat just outside the door.

His heart swelled up to twice its normal size to find her waiting there. "You stayed."

She smiled. "I did. What's the verdict?"

"Not guilty." He grabbed her and swung her around, laughing. "I'm not an ignoramus after all. I just needed a little more color in my life. Can you believe it? I swear it's a miracle." He held up the envelope JoAnna had given him. "All I have to do is put a purple sheet and a turquoise sheet of plastic over a page, and I can read it. Olivia, I can *read* it. The letters don't jiggle or dance or run together. The words just sit there and let me read them.'' He laughed and swung her around again. ''Let's go home. This calls for champagne!''

Eleven

Olivia was dressed and waiting when she heard boots hit the bottom stairs. She and Jackson had parted at UT just over an hour before with his admonition to go home and get her glad rags on. They were going out to celebrate. She smiled thinking of his exuberance. She'd never seen him so deliriously happy.

"Open up, woman!" Jackson shouted. "My arms are full."

She threw open the door to a beaming Jackson with armloads of flowers—red roses, yellow roses, magnificent lilies and a huge potted orchid.

"Good heavens! Did you buy out the florist?"

"Just about. I'd already gotten the roses when I remembered that you once said you liked this kind of lily—"

"They're stargazers," she supplied, laughing as

she caught his infectious mood. ''And they're beautiful.''

''Right. Stargazers. And you went on so over that pot of orchids at the Chinese restaurant last week that I got the same kind for you. I would have brought more stuff, but this is all I could carry.'' He kissed her, then said, ''Grab the pot, will you, darlin'? I've got a thorn sticking my finger.''

She took the orchid along with the bundle of lilies and started to the kitchen, wondering what in the world she was going to use for vases. After a bit of searching, she found containers that would do.

The huge bouquet of red roses went into the single large vase she owned, a cut glass one that she'd picked up on a junking spree. The two dozen yellow roses went into a tall pickle crock, and the lilies into a blue glass pitcher.

When she'd finished with the overwhelming mass, Jackson was still beaming. He seemed so excited that she didn't dare mention that he might have gone a tad overboard. ''The flowers are lovely, and they smell heavenly. Thank you.''

Wrapping his arms around her, he laid his forehead against hers. ''I know I got a little carried away, sugar, but I owe you a lot more that an armload of flowers for what you've done for me. Do you have any idea what a difference you've made in my life? I couldn't repay you if I gave you every flower in Texas.''

He reached into his pocket and pulled out a small box wrapped in gold paper. ''I want you to have this, too.''

She frowned. ''Jackson—''

"Now, darlin', don't go getting on your high horse like you do every time I try to give you something. This is a red-letter day for me. You can't imagine how it feels to know that I'm not really stupid, that I can read a book now like a normal person, that I don't have to fake my way through every single day. Please, honey. I want you to have this. Okay?"

The expression on his face was so tender and so entreating that her heart simply melted. "Okay." She tore away the paper and opened the small box. A pair of exquisite diamond studs sparkled against the dark velvet interior.

"But, Jackson, I can't accept these. They're huge. They must have cost a fortune."

"Naw. I charged 'em."

A smile escaped her despite her best efforts. "I appreciate the thought, I really do, but I can't accept these."

"Too late. You already said okay. Here, let's put them on, and we're going to go out for a champagne dinner. There's that fancy place outside town that we haven't tried yet. I think I mentioned it to you. They serve wild game of all kinds and pour a whiskey sauce over ice cream that'll make you swear you've died and gone to heaven."

Olivia didn't argue any more. This was a special day for Jackson, and she didn't want to spoil it for him. She took off her plain gold loops and laid them in the kitchen window. Standing in front of a small wall mirror in the living room, she inserted the studs, then turned around for his reaction.

"Beautiful, absolutely beautiful. I knew you were made for diamonds." He pulled another gold-wrapped package from his coat pocket. This one was longer and narrow. "Here."

"No."

"But, darlin'—"

"No. Absolutely not. The earrings are too much."

He caught her around the waist and penned her in his arms. After a small kiss and a nuzzle, he asked, "Aren't you even curious?"

"Not in the least. I'm not going to take another expensive gift."

"What if I told you it was just a fountain pen?" He nuzzled the other ear and nipped at the lobe.

"I wouldn't believe you. I thought you were taking me to dinner. I'm starved."

"Oh, can't have that, sugar. Where's your coat? It's nippy outside."

Jackson was like a kid when he whipped out his colored overlays and placed them over the menu. "Looka there, I can read every word. You want rattlesnake or wild boar?"

She wrinkled her nose.

"Don't worry about it, darlin'. I promise that everything here is de-licious and like nothing you've ever tasted before. They floosy it up so that you don't even know what you're eating half the time. How about venison?"

"You want me to *eat* Bambi?"

"Sorry, sugar, bad choice. Ever tried alligator? How about duck? That's not too different from chicken."

"Why don't you order for me? Just whisper it to the waiter so I won't know."

He grinned, but he ended up doing just that. When the waiter left, he picked up his glass of champagne and touched it to hers. "To a remarkable lady, and to the future."

"To new horizons," she added, then sipped from her glass.

He drank also, then he sat holding his glass and simply watching her for the longest time.

"What?"

"I was just thinking how bright you are. And how beautiful. And how much I love you."

Her breath caught, and she looked quickly away. This wasn't supposed to happen. She hadn't wanted this to happen. She didn't want declarations and commitments. She wasn't ready.

"Honey, don't look at me like that."

"Like what?"

"Like you're about to panic and start circling the wagons. I just said what I felt. I'm not pushing."

She turned her glass round and round, then took another sip. "When are you going to get colored filters?"

He sighed, then said, "I'll call the closest place in the morning and go in as soon as they can take me. I'm mighty anxious to get those glasses."

Olivia was relieved that he didn't mention the *L* word any more, not even when he came to her bed later that night.

Her apartment smelled of roses and lilies and desire when he kissed her and caressed her and unzipped her dress slowly. She savored each moment, returned every caress and unbuttoned his shirt to touch his bare skin.

Their lovemaking was slow and sweet and sensuous. Her body sang to his whispers, swelled under his seduction and slipped over the edge of the world with wonderful racking spasms of fulfillment.

She snuggled close, content in his arms, taking comfort from his size and strength and slept.

"Darlin'," he whispered, waking her from a lovely dream, "it's morning. I've gotta go."

She roused only to smile and flutter her fingers.

He chuckled and kissed the back of her neck. "I'll set your alarm."

She fluttered her fingers again and didn't move until the alarm jerked her awake. She smacked it off and rolled back onto her stomach, bunching and hugging the pillow under her head.

Her hand encountered something hard beneath the pillow, and she patted it, trying to figure out what it was. Pulling out the object, she raised up and squinted at it.

The other gold-wrapped box.

Pushing back her tumbled hair, she squinted at it some more.

Dare she?

No. Absolutely not.

She put the box on her bedside table and went to the bathroom to brush her teeth.

Curiosity itched inside her. She peered around the door and saw the box still sitting there. Tearing her gaze away, she scrubbed her teeth harder.

She dressed and made her bed and tried not to think about that box. She carried it to the kitchen with her when she fixed coffee.

The coffee seemed to take forever to drip. She leaned over, put her elbows on the counter and her chin in her hands. Her eyes went from the slow drip-drip of brewing coffee to the box. The package seemed to beckon her.

"Oh, go for it!" She snatched up the package and tore off the wrapping paper.

She gasped when she opened the box. It was a diamond tennis bracelet—five carats at least. A small gold tag was attached near the clasp. Something was engraved on it. Holding it close to the light, she read the three words.

I love you.

She sank to the floor and wept.

Dear Lord, she loved him, too.

Olivia was about to leave for the university when the phone rang.

"Hey, sugar, I'm glad I caught you," Jackson said. "I'm on my way to the airport. The soonest I could get an appointment at an Irlen Clinic is this afternoon at one o'clock in Houston, so I'm going to fly down. I have some other business to tend to, so I'll be gone until Friday afternoon."

"You certainly move fast."

"You betcha. I wanted to go to the head honcho's place in California, except they can't see me for two weeks. With this deal, I'll come home with the glasses."

"I hope this solves your problem. You know that this might only be part of your difficulty."

"I know, I know. JoAnna briefed me on all that,

and she gave me a book. I'm going to read it on the plane.''

Olivia smiled at the pride in his voice. ''That's great.''

''Listen, sugar, I'm almost at the airport. Would you do a couple of things for me?''

''Sure. What?''

''Would you check on Streak at night? Let him out for a run and give him food and water. Mrs. Lopez will tend to him while she's there.''

''No problem. What's the second thing?''

''Call Irish and tell her that their suites are confirmed at the Driskill for this weekend and that I have a tee time at eight on Saturday morning for Kyle and Matt and me to play golf with Mitch. She can pass on the word to Eve and Matt.''

''Will do.''

''I've gotta go, darlin'. Call you tonight. Love you.''

He hung up before she could reply.

She'd almost forgotten about the special weekend coming up. The president's reception at the governor's mansion. What in the world was she going to wear? she wondered as she punched in Irish's Dallas number. Her choices were severely limited. Maybe Irish had some ideas.

She did.

''Oh, heavens, Olivia, you can't wear that old bridesmaid dress,'' Irish said. ''I have a closet full of gowns, some of them with the tags still on, and I'm already too poochy to wear them. In fact, I have one in mind that would be perfect for you, but I'll bring along two or three to try. Would you believe that I even convinced Eve to buy a new dress for the occasion? I can hardly wait to get there. We're flying in Friday afternoon after Kyle gets through at the hospital."

"Wonderful," Olivia said. "We can get together Saturday morning while the guys play golf."

"Count on it. And Friday night for dinner, too."

"If Jackson gets in from Houston in time."

"What's Jackson doing in Houston?"

"Business," Olivia said quickly. She didn't dare reveal his secret, even now.

"Are things heating up between you two?"

"It depends on how you define heat," Olivia said, trying not to giggle.

"Oh, I think we define it pretty much the same way, m'dear. Is there a serious romance blooming?"

"Oh, I wouldn't call it…too serious. You know Jackson. He's not the serious type. And neither am I. We enjoy each other's company. Say, how's the morning sickness these days?" she asked, steering the conversation in a different direction. They chatted for another minute or two, then Olivia said, "I could yak all day, but I have to run. I have a seminar."

The days crawled by slowly. Even though she was busy, Olivia discovered just how much Jackson had insinuated himself into her life. Without him around, there was a big, empty space.

The second evening that he was gone, she went across the street to play with Streak and feed him. The puppy seemed lonely, too. He looked at her with such pitiful eyes that she stayed longer to keep him company. They watched a movie on TV, she on the couch and Streak on her lap. She hadn't meant to fall asleep, but she did. She awoke at two o'clock in the morning, Streak still curled against her and an infomercial on the TV.

Darn it! She'd missed Jackson's phone call. He'd called the night before to tell her that his exam had gone well, and his glasses should be ready on Friday afternoon. He'd be flying in as soon as he picked them up.

Olivia dialed her own number to see if he'd left a message.

He'd left four.

The last one was at one-thirty. "Where are you, darlin'? I'm worried about you. Call me when you get in."

Should she or shouldn't she?

She should. She tucked a warm throw around her and called his hotel. He answered on the first ring.

"I'm sorry to call so late, but I fell asleep on your couch."

"You gave me a scare. I was afraid something had happened to you."

"Nope. Streak and I watched a movie."

"John Wayne?"

She chuckled. "Not on your life. It was a very urbane romantic comedy. I only wish I knew how it ended."

"They lived happily ever after," he said. "Isn't that the way they always end?"

"In movies." A sudden melancholy swept over her, clogging her throat and bringing a sting of tears to her eyes. "Real life doesn't always work that way."

"It does if the two people involved want to make it work. I want us to live happily ever after. Don't you?"

A glib answer died on her lips. What did she want? Was there a future for Jackson and her? She tried to picture it and couldn't. At least she didn't panic thinking about it, but she wasn't ready to promise any lasting commitments, either.

"I won't crowd you, sugar," Jackson said after the long silence. "But I can't help but wonder sometimes just how you feel about me."

"I care very deeply about you, Jackson."

"Do I hear a *but* in there?"

She let out a slow breath and stroked the puppy's soft fur while she thought about her answer.

"Darlin'?"

"I think you deserve to know about my past, and perhaps someday I'll tell you the whole story, but not tonight. It's late and we both need to get some sleep. The short version is that I've been abused by the men in my life, and it makes me very cautious."

"Olivia, I would cut off my right arm before I would ever harm a hair on your head. I swear by all that's holy. Trust me, darlin'. I love you."

Deep down, she knew what Jackson said was true. Even so, she could feel tiny fingers of panic starting to unfurl as he pursued the issue. She loved him, too, but she wasn't ready to say the words, nor was she ready make the commitment that went with them. Not yet. Not yet.

Maybe not ever.

"Are you going to be home in time to have dinner with Irish and Kyle and Eve and Matt?" she asked.

She heard only the barest of sighs from the phone. ''Yes. I talked to Matt this evening. Everybody's coming over to my house, and we're going to keep things casual. Six-thirty okay with you?''

''Fine,'' she said, yawning. ''Do you need me to do anything?''

''No, but thanks for offering. Tami arranged for a caterer to handle stuff. Darlin', would you do a favor for me?''

''Sure. What?''

''I don't want you out alone this time of night. Why don't you stay there and go to bed.''

''Jackson, my place is just across the street.''

''Humor me.''

She smiled. ''Okay. I'll stay.''

''Dream of me,'' he whispered.

Twelve

Olivia felt like Cinderella as their group rode in a long and imposing black limousine to the governor's mansion in downtown Austin. The six of them had enjoyed their casual get-together the evening before at Jackson's, and on Saturday, while the men played golf, the women had primped for the occasion. She could hardly believe that the same bunch that had eaten fried chicken in their jeans one night could be turned out like fashion plates to share paté with the president and the first lady the next. Well, everybody except Eve, of course. Irish's younger sister was a vegetarian.

The sapphire panne velvet dress that Irish had insisted was perfect for Olivia, was. Its lines, from the bateau neckline to the hem that just touched the floor, were simple but elegant and the long sleeves were comfortable for the cool November evening. Irish had even insisted on loaning her a spectacular diamond and sapphire pin that set off the dress perfectly. And she wore the diamond studs that Jackson had given her.

But not the bracelet. As beautiful as it was, she was going to return it to him. She simply hadn't had a chance. The only moment they'd had alone was when he picked her up at her apartment—and the others were waiting downstairs in the limo.

"You look scrumptious, sweetheart," he'd said when she'd opened the door. "Fantastic! That dress matches your eyes exactly."

She beamed and her hand automatically went to her upswept hairdo. Borrowing the gown and spending most of the afternoon with Irish and Eve in Austin's finest beauty salon had paid off. They had gotten the works: fabulous hair styling, manicures and facials. Even her toenails were painted siren red. Eve had groused the whole time, but Olivia had enjoyed it. She'd felt positively decadent.

As Jackson put the matching wrap around her shoulders, he'd kissed her nape and whispered, "How about you and me skip this shindig and stay home in bed?"

"Not on your life, buster. I didn't go to this much trouble to spend the evening in the dark."

He'd grinned. "We can leave the lights on."

"I don't think so," she'd said, picking up her evening bag. "Let's go see the president and the first lady. By the way, how are the new glasses working out?"

"Great. They're even better than the overlays. And,

uh, sugar, I haven't told Matt and Kyle about…you know."

"Then I won't tell them, either." She'd given him a quick kiss on the cheek before they went downstairs to join the others.

Now the limo was pulling up to the front of the stately governor's mansion with its huge white columns and view of the state capitol and grounds. The place was ablaze with lights and thick with security.

Irish and Kyle were the first out of the limo, then Eve and Matt. Jackson climbed out and offered her his hand, smiling as she exited the car.

Cherokee Pete would have been proud of his grandsons, three handsome men in their tuxedos going to meet the president of the United States. Irish was gorgeous in an emerald-green suit with a floor-length skirt and a boxy beaded jacket to accommodate the first signs of her pregnancy, and Eve was equally beautiful in a dusky-rose silk gown.

Jackson tucked Olivia's arm in his, and, after they passed through a security check at the gate, they started up the walkway with the others. She felt like a movie star, smiling and girlishly giddy as cameras flashed around them.

Inside, she actually met the president and the first lady, though later she couldn't for the life of her remember what she'd said to them. She hoped it was something sensible.

Mitch had hugged her, and Jackson had glared at him. They nibbled from the bountifully filled buffet tables and chatted with the movers and shakers in attendance. Jackson seemed to know everyone—and those he didn't know, he quickly befriended.

He was a charmer, no doubt about it. Men liked him, and women grew more animated when he was around. And she thought his new glasses made him look more distinguished.

Matt had noticed the glasses first thing. "Had to break down and get some cheaters, huh, big brother?"

"We're all getting older, fly boy," was all Jackson had said.

The evening passed in a whirl of introductions and conversations, and before Olivia knew it, it was time to leave.

At Irish's insistence they all stopped by the hotel to have a nightcap. Olivia had fallen in love with the historic old Driskill with its Romanesque exterior and sumptuous Victorian interiors. The bar was a huge room done in a Western motif with overstuffed leather sofas, ranch paintings and a stuffed longhorn head over the fireplace.

"Gruesome, isn't it," Eve said, shuddering and sitting with her back to the steer head.

"Sweetheart, not everybody is the animal lover that you are," Matt said. To Olivia he said, "Would you believe that not only do we have two cats, four dogs and an aria-singing parrot, we have a *pig* as a house pet?"

She laughed. "I understand that pigs are very bright."

"Minerva is extremely bright," Eve said. "And neater than Matt." She winked at her husband.

After everyone ordered drinks, Irish said, "I almost forgot to mention it, Olivia, but Kyle and I are having Thanksgiving at our house this year. I hope you'll come with Jackson. We'd really love to have you.

Everybody is pitching in, and it will be so much fun. We're doing the turkey, Grandpa Pete is making cornbread dressing and gravy, Mother is making pumpkin pies, Kyle's mother is providing vegetables—"

"And we're bringing homemade bread and butter," Eve added.

"Mom and Dad are springing for the wine," Matt said.

"Mom doesn't cook anymore," Jackson added, "not since they live in the hotel."

"I didn't realize that your parents lived in a hotel," Olivia said.

"Mmm-hmm. In San Antonio. They own it and live in the penthouse when they're in town. They travel a lot. Where are they now, Matt? I forget."

"I think the last postcard we got was from Japan. They should be on their way home about now."

"Well, anyhow, Olivia," Irish said. "I hope you'll come."

"Sure she will," Jackson said.

"What can I bring?"

Jackson grinned. "She makes a mean coconut cake."

"Great!" Kyle said. "Coconut is my favorite."

Irish rolled her eyes. "Any kind of cake is your favorite."

"Can I help it if I have a sweet tooth?" He leaned over and playfully gnawed on Irish's shoulder.

Olivia laughed at the bantering of the two couples who were obviously so much in love. She wondered if it was wise to spend the holiday with the families. She had a premonition that there would be a lot of matchmaking going on.

After they finished their drinks, Olivia and Jackson said their farewells and rode home in the limousine. Jackson had the driver drop them off at his house.

"My bed *is* roomier," he said as he unlocked the door, "and I've been itching to unzip that dress all night."

They were barely inside when he tossed her wrap aside, pulled her into his arms and kissed her. She felt his fingers at her back and the slow slide of the zipper as he drew it down. She shivered and melted against him.

Their tongues met and their moans mingled and her dress fell into a puddle around her feet.

His jacket joined it. Then his tie and cummerbund.

His studs and her shoes were scattered along the path to his bedroom.

"New undies, I see," Jackson said as he kissed her shoulder and unclasped her bra.

"Mmm. Irish and Eve talked me into buying them at Victoria's Secret. They matched the dress. Like them?"

"Love them." He tossed the bra across the room. Her panties landed on top of the lamp. "I think garter belts are sexy. Remind me to buy stock in Victoria's Secret."

She slipped off his shirt and ran her tongue along his collarbone.

His boots landed with a *thud, thud,* and he shucked his pants and hung them on the bedpost. The last of his clothes landed in a heap near the chair.

"I've never made love to a woman wearing only stockings and a garter belt, but I always thought it would be a turn-on. Saw a picture in a magazine when I was a kid, and I've fantasized about it ever since."

"You told me, and I remembered."

"Did you now?" He circled her nipple with his tongue, then sucked gently.

She gasped at the sensation. "I did. Nobody wears garter belts with stockings much anymore."

He laid her on the bed and stroked up the length of her leg. "They should. It feels sensational."

He kissed her and stroked her and touched her until she was begging him to enter. At last he slipped into place and plunged deeply. He moved slowly at first, but she urged him on, and the pace quickened.

Their rhythm was wild and sensuous, and their climaxes powerful.

When the last shudder had stilled, Jackson ran his hand up one of her stockinged legs and over the garter belt.

"Darlin', I may have these bronzed."

On Sunday morning they lay in bed, sipping coffee and reading the papers.

"I still can't believe this," Jackson said. "I'm actually *reading* a newspaper. It's amazing. Oh, I'm going to have to have some extra tutoring for a while to improve my skills, but, dammit, I'm actually *reading*. And looka here, sugar, our pictures are in the Austin paper."

"Where?" She craned her neck to peer at the section he held.

"Right here in living color. There's a write-up about the president's reception." Very slowly and deliberately he read: "'From left to right—Dr. Kyle

Rutledge and his wife Irish, the former New York model. Matthew Crow of Crow Airlines and his wife Eve, Dallas ad executive. Olivia Moore, university professor, and Jackson Crow, railroad commissioner.' ''

''Let me see that. I'm not a professor! I'm merely an instructor.''

He grinned. ''Wanna sue?''

''I'll pass. That's an excellent picture. I wish I had a copy.''

''I'll check with the newspaper office. Maybe I can wangle one out of them.'' He touched the picture, then ran his finger over the caption. ''You know, it's a miracle, Olivia. With these colored filters I can actually see your name. It's so beautiful.''

Tenderness filled her, and she rubbed her cheek against his. Things were just about perfect.

Olivia was in her living room grading term projects and half listening to the evening news on TV, when ''president'' and ''Austin'' caught her attention. She looked up and saw the last of a story about the president's vacation in Texas and the Saturday reception at the governor's mansion. There was a film clip of Mitch and the president and the first lady receiving guests, and—ohmygod! There she was! And there was Jackson and the others.

Panic rushed over her. What if Thomas saw that? She'd been so careful to lie low and cover her trail, and now here she was on television. Slapping her hand on her chest, she forced herself to breathe deeply and relax. But panic clawed at her insides. Her picture in the local paper had made her uneasy; seeing herself on television was horrifying.

When she realized that she'd been watching a local newscast, she sighed with relief. It was highly unlikely that Thomas Fairchild, in California, had access to Austin newspapers or TV broadcasts.

Keep calm, Olivia, she told herself. Thomas wasn't going to find her. In all probability he had given up on her by now and moved on with his life.

She hoped.

No matter how much positive self-talk she used, a niggling doubt lingered and worried a corner of her mind.

She slept poorly that night and awoke early to sit in her rocking chair, her gown tucked around her toes, and stare into space. And she prayed.

When the phone rang, she almost jumped out of her skin.

It was Irish.

"Have you been watching CNN?" Irish asked.

"No. Why?"

"We're on. They have a film clip of the president's visit to Austin and all of us shaking hands with him at the reception. Isn't that neat?"

Olivia's mouth went dry. "No, Irish. It's not neat."

There was dead silence for a moment.

"Thomas," Irish said.

"Thomas."

"Oh, Lord, Olivia, I'm sorry. But I'm sure you don't need to worry. Even if he sees the film, he might not realize that it was you. I mean, you were only on for a fraction of a second. I recognized the dress first. And you aren't identified in any way. You've changed your name, and your phone is unlisted. It's unlikely that he'll find you."

"Unlikely. That's what I've told myself."

"Olivia, have you told Jackson about Thomas?"

"No, not really."

"Tell him, sweetie. Tell him and let him protect you."

"I'll think about it."

"We'll talk more when you come to Dallas. When are you arriving?"

"We'll be driving up Wednesday afternoon and staying in a hotel. We'll see you Thursday morning."

"Oh, I wanted you to stay with us. We have scads of room in this big house."

Olivia smiled when she recalled Jackson's reaction to the suggestion. Not no, but "Hell, no," he'd said. "That place will be like fleas on a farm dog with all the relatives coming in. Let's stay where we can have some privacy."

"But I suppose you two would rather have a place with more privacy," Irish said.

"Those were almost Jackson's exact words."

Time dragged by, and Olivia was exhausted by the time she returned home Tuesday afternoon. It seemed that everyone she'd met for the past two days had seen her picture in the paper or on television. Apprehension and lack of sleep had her nerves on edge.

The phone rang.

She started and cried out at the sudden sound. Her hand hovered over the receiver, and it rang again.

It was probably Jackson. Or Tessa. Or Irish.

It rang again.

She snatched it up.

"Hello?"

Nothing.

"Hello?" she repeated, louder. After the third hello, she slammed the phone down and rubbed her arms to ward off a prickly chill.

Thomas, the frightened part of her said. *Wrong number,* her stoic self said.

The phone rang again. She reached for it but couldn't make herself pick up the receiver. Instead she let the answering machine click on. Ed Jurney's deep voice said, "This is 555-6304. Leave a message and we'll call you back."

Thank heavens that Ed, for security's sake, had made the recording for her when she'd first moved in.

"Hey, darlin', it's me," Jackson said. "I'm going to have to work late—"

She snatched up the phone. "I'm here."

"Good. I was afraid that I'd missed you."

"Did you call before?"

"Before now? No. I have another hour or two's work to do here, and I didn't want you to wait on me for dinner. Mrs. Lopez said there was one of those casserole things that you like in the refrigerator. She said all we have to do is heat it up and toss a salad to go with it. Go ahead and eat, and I'll eat when I get home. And, babe, would you mind taking care of Streak?"

"Not at all. And I'll wait for you. I'm sorry you have to work late."

"Everybody wants to get off early for the holiday,

so we're trying to finish up some things. Gotta go, sugar. Love you.''

He was gone before she could say anything else—not that she would have confided her fears. This was something that she would deal with. Thomas was her problem, her nemesis, her nightmare.

Familiar anxiety began to build inside her.

If he hadn't seen the TV clip, she was sure some mutual acquaintance would have seen it and told him about it. Pretending that she was safe was a fantasy. Hadn't he told her that last time? Hadn't he shouted, as she hid behind a neighbor's shrubbery, that she could never escape him? Hadn't he tracked her and almost caught her three times?

She grabbed the stack of student papers from her desk and fled her apartment. She ran across the street, unlocked Jackson's front door, then reset the alarm and dead-bolted the heavy door behind her.

But she couldn't lock out the memories or outrun the fears. They followed her inside. She could never forget that night.

Thomas had beaten her before, once so badly that she had to be hospitalized. She'd told the doctor that she'd been attacked when she surprised a burglar. She'd had to lie. Thomas was standing at the foot of the gurney—acting like a loving, overwrought husband—and had threatened to kill her if she didn't lie. Anyhow, who would have believed that Thomas Fairchild would have done such a thing? He was a federal judge, highly respected in the town. He played golf with the mayor and the chief of police…and her own father. Besides, everyone knew that he adored his wife, doted on her.

In his own sick way, he had loved her. And in the beginning she'd loved him, too, but as their marriage deteriorated, as his abuse escalated, her love had quickly died.

She'd tried many times to leave him, but he always found her and brought her back. Twice, when she'd fled to her childhood home, her father, the bastard, had called Thomas and told him where she was. Thomas was always contrite after one of his outbursts, begging her to forgive him, showering her with gifts, proclaiming his deep love for her. Things would be fine for a while. He would be the perfect husband—loving, tender, considerate. Then something would set him off again.

She was sensible enough to realize that his abuse wasn't going to end, but she was terrified of the man. And with good reason. Controlling her in every way, he'd made her an emotional cripple. The mere mention of her getting a job would send him into a tirade. She never had more than a few dollars in cash, nor did she have access to their bank accounts. Oh, he'd been generous with her, but everything had to be charged, and she knew that he could cut off her credit with a phone call. He kept the most costly of her jewelry in a safe in his study, not trusting her with the combination, but taking out pieces as she needed to wear them—even the things that had been her mother's.

But she'd learned to be devious. She searched until she found the combination to the safe. She began stockpiling cash, charging lunch with friends and taking their money, returning purchases and getting cash. A little here and a little there began to add up. She hid it in an old purse in the back of her closet, waiting for her chance.

That last night, she'd finally screwed up enough courage to tell Thomas that she was divorcing him. He'd grown wild with rage, slapped her to the floor, then dragged her back up and shaken her, shouted obscenities and struck her again. He threw her against a wall mirror and her head shattered the heavy glass.

"You'll never leave me, Olivia. You're *mine!* No other man will ever touch you. I'll see you dead first."

When he reached for the fireplace poker, Olivia knew that he meant to kill her. Somehow she'd found the strength to run from the house. Keeping to the shadows, she'd hidden behind the oleanders at the Almont's house, a block away.

She'd waited there for hours, bruised and bleeding and terrified, until she saw Thomas leave in his car. She'd hurried back to the house and grabbed money, jewelry and what she could fit into her car and fled.

She hadn't stopped running.

A coldness rippled over her and set her to shivering.

He was going to find her. She knew it.

Her instincts told her to run. Fast and far away.

Thirteen

Olivia didn't relax until they were on the freeway headed to Dallas. Even then, she kept looking behind them to see if anyone was following the car.

"Sugar, what's the matter with you? For the last few days, you've been jumpier than a cricket in a hot skillet."

"Just nervous about the prospect of being around all your relatives, I suppose."

He reached for her hand, squeezing it. "No need to worry about that. You've already met and charmed every one of them. Mama even said she brought you a present from Japan."

"Jackson, your parents don't think that we—"

"That we—what?"

"I mean, they're not expecting us to get engaged or anything like that, are they?"

He was quiet for a moment, then said, ''We haven't discussed it.''

She relaxed a bit more. For the next few days she was going to forget about her worries and enjoy herself. It was unlikely that Thomas would track her to Dallas, and she would be surrounded by powerful people. Even if he did find her, he wouldn't dare try to harm her.

No, he'd wait until he had her alone.

The bustle of preparing Thanksgiving dinner—which was served at noon rather than in the evening—kept Olivia's mind off her worries about Thomas. Jackson's parents, Anna and Sam Crow, had brought everyone, including Olivia, lovely silk robes from their trip to Japan. The men's were emblazoned with embroidered dragons and the women's with exquisite flowers and birds.

She really liked Jackson's parents, who, despite over forty years of marriage, still appeared to be very much in love. They were a striking couple, both tall with dark eyes and dark hair going gray, his more than hers. Anna looked very much like her sister, Sarah Rutledge, Kyle's mother, though Sarah's hair was lighter. Both had an ageless sort of beauty with their wonderful high cheekbones and sculpted features that were part of their native American ancestry.

Kyle shared his blond coloring with his father, who had blue eyes and light hair that was now almost white. Dr. T. J. Rutledge was a cardiologist, newly retired. Since they were both heart specialists, Olivia would have bet that T.J. had met her father at one medical convention or another through the years, but she didn't dare ask.

Irish and Eve's parents, Beverly and Al Ellison, both as tall and fair as their daughters, were as warm and welcoming as they'd always been. They loved being new Texans, and Al especially bragged on the mild climate of their adopted state and his skills as a fisherman on the lake where they'd retired.

When the food was ready, everyone gathered around Irish and Kyle's massive dining table. By popular request Cherokee Pete sat at the head. After leading the Thanksgiving prayer, he and Kyle carved two huge turkeys.

Since Irish had given her housekeeper the day off, the meal was served family style, and food was plentiful. It seemed that everybody had brought extra things, and bowls and platters were passed around amid laughter and joking.

"Oops," Irish said, rising. "I forgot the cranberry sauce. It's in the fridge."

"I'll get it," Kyle said. "Stay off your feet."

When the turkey was served and the plates were heaped with dressing and green beans and sweet potatoes and salads and a half dozen other dishes, Jackson said, "Maybe I'd better use one of those platters. I'm running out of room."

His father laughed and agreed, as did Al Ellison.

"I'm planning on seconds," Matt said.

"Save plenty of room for dessert," Sam Crow said. "I've had my eye on that coconut cake Olivia brought."

"Me, too," Kyle said, "but I plan to have cake and pie both."

Irish laughed. ‘‘You would.’’

Gaiety and the drone of congenial conversation filled the large room and sparked warm fuzzies inside Olivia.

She looked around at all those gathered—the whole clan except for Jackson’s sister and her family and Kyle’s brother. They were such likable people, warm, funny, down-to-earth despite their wealth. They had opened their arms and made her feel welcome. Strange. She felt more a part of this group than she’d ever felt at home.

Family meals had usually been an ordeal when she was growing up. More often than not, her father would go into one of his tirades about some infraction or another. After her mother had died, Jason had been his whipping boy, but Olivia had endured many of her father’s tongue-lashings as well. And after Jason left, there had been no buffer between Olivia and her father’s vitriolic eruptions. She had become his only target. Yet, as controlling and emotionally abusive as her father had been, he hadn’t hit her as often as he had hit Jason, in all likelihood because she had tiptoed around her home like a mouse. On the other hand, Thomas—

No, she told herself, no thinking about Thomas. Not now. She focused her attention back on those gathered in the dining room. It was then that she realized thirteen people were at the table. Bad luck if you believed such things.

A shiver went over her.

‘‘Olivia, what’s wrong?’’ Jackson asked.

‘‘Nothing,’’ she said with a nervous laugh. ‘‘I just realized that I’m the thirteenth person.’’

"Nope," Irish piped up. She patted her tummy. "He makes fourteen."

"Do you know that it's a *he?*" her mother asked.

Irish nodded and caught Kyle's hand. "We were going to wait until dessert to make the announcement, but—"

"But we're having a son," Kyle finished, beaming.

Cherokee Pete rose and lifted his wineglass. "I'd like to propose a toast to our family's new additions. To my new great-grandson and to our most welcome friend, Olivia."

"Hear, hear!"

Olivia felt herself blush, but she also felt her heart expand. She'd never realized just how much she'd missed in not being part of a large and loving family.

That awareness grew when, after the meal, the men rushed to the den to watch the Dallas Cowboys football game, leaving the women to clean up the mess.

"Male chauvinist pigs," Eve shouted after them, laughing after she said it.

Anna Crow laughed as well. "They're all like little boys. Never," she told Olivia, "get between one of these men and a Cowboys game. They're all die-hard fans, always have been."

"That's the truth," Irish said. "They have season tickets to all the games. Only on threat of death did they forgo being there in person today."

Olivia smiled and pitched in to clear the table, but she realized that this was probably the first Cowboys game Jackson had watched this season. He'd spent all his Sunday afternoons with Tami, preparing for the commission's Monday hearings and suffering blinding headaches. Jackson was truly dedicated to doing his job well. Her admiration for him rose another notch.

The weekend in Dallas seemed to fly by, and Olivia thoroughly enjoyed herself. The day after Thanksgiving, they went out to see the new farmhouse that Matt and Eve were building, and she got to meet Minerva, the wonder pig, as well as all Eve's other animals.

She and Jackson spent time with his family and managed to squeeze in some time on their own as well. On Saturday night they went to a performance of a Broadway musical on tour, drank wine and made love.

On Sunday morning they started home.

Fears that had been suspended for the holiday suddenly recurred with a wallop. The closer they came to Austin, the more her anxiety grew.

By the time Jackson carried her bags upstairs to her apartment, dread filled her stomach like a hot stone.

"Darlin', are you okay?"

"I'm fine," she said, forcing a smile. "Just tired. But I had a lovely time. I really like your family."

"And they like you." He dropped her bags in her living room and took her in his arms. "I do, too."

He brushed noses with her, then kissed her. She wanted to hold on to him forever, but she knew he had work to do.

"Get some rest this afternoon," he told her, "and I'll call you later."

When he had gone, she hurried to her answering machine and checked messages. Four hang ups and a call from Tessa playfully asking for a report on the weekend.

Four hang ups.

Probably wrong numbers or randomly dialed computer calls trying to sell her something.

Probably. After all, her number was unlisted.

But Thomas was a judge, friends with police officials and others who could easily secure unlisted numbers.

She locked the door carefully, using both dead bolt and chain as a backup, and took three slow deep breaths. Then she unpacked and called Tessa.

Tessa wasn't home. After leaving a message on her machine, she went to fix a cup of hot tea. She couldn't seem to get warm.

The phone rang.

She hesitated a moment, then picked it up. "Hello."

Silence.

"Hello! Hello! Dammit, who's there?"

"Ah, so it is you."

Olivia's heart almost stopped, and she ceased to breathe. Her blood ran ice-cold.

Thomas.

Her worst nightmare had just become real.

"What do you want?" she asked, trying to remain calm.

"I want what I've always wanted. You, at home with me where you belong."

"I don't belong with you, Thomas. We're divorced."

"You do belong with me, Olivia. You're *mine!* You'll always be *mine*. I'm coming to pick you up."

Trembling with panic, she ran to the kitchen window, terrified that he might be outside. "I'm not going anywhere with you, Thomas. We're divorced. Leave me alone."

"I saw you on television, and I saw the newspaper picture of you with that bastard's hands on you. He can't have you, Olivia. You belong to *me*. I'll be coming for you. You'll leave with me, or I'll see you dead."

She broke the connection and flung the phone aside. Grabbing the edge of the sink, she held on tightly and clenched her teeth as her body shook. *No,* she prayed. *No, please no.*

Run! Run! She had to pack her bags and get out of there before he came. He said he'd kill her, and she knew that he would.

She glanced up and saw Jackson's house across the street. If she called him, he'd be there in an instant. Thomas would be no match for Jackson Crow.

Or would he? Thomas might have a gun, and as furious as he was, he would shoot Jackson with the slightest provocation. Thomas had always been violently jealous, even when there was no reason, and he was an excellent shot. Jackson might be killed if she called him.

A sudden calm moved over her, and she stood straight and tall. No, she wasn't calling Jackson, nor was she going to run away. She was done with running. She was making her stand here. Now.

A car stopped in the driveway, a big luxury car. Thomas Fairchild got out.

Her stomach tightened, but for the most part, Olivia remained calm. She picked up the phone and dialed

911. Her voice was shaky, but she managed. After giving her name and address, she said, "My ex-husband has just threatened to murder me, and he's walking up to the door now. Hurry. For God's sake, hurry!"

"We've dispatched a car," the woman said. "Stay on the line and don't open the door."

"You couldn't pay me to open it. I hear him walking up the steps to my apartment. Oh, God, he's coming!"

"A car is less than a minute away. Hold on."

Thomas knocked on the door. "Olivia!"

When she didn't answer, he banged on it. "Olivia! Open the door!" After a moment he banged again, harder. "You're *mine,* dammit, and you're coming with me!"

"Don't open the door," the dispatcher warned.

"I'm not crazy," she whispered.

"You're coming with me, or I'll kill you! I swear I will. No other man is having what's mine!" The door shuddered as he threw his weight against it.

"He's trying to break down the door," she whispered. "Go away, Thomas!" she shouted. "I've called the police."

"You're lying. Open up! Now!" He hit the door like a battering ram.

The power of his fury shook her to the core, but she clenched her teeth and strengthened her resolve. She'd never reported him to the police before, and he thought she was the same cowed woman she used to be. She wasn't. If she went down, this time she'd go down fighting.

Wood splintered, the glass in the door shattered.

Olivia picked up a pewter candlestick, preparing to defend herself. "He's coming in!" she shouted, running to the door and smashing her candlestick against the hand that reached through the broken pane and tried to unlock the dead bolt.

A siren came screaming down the street. Two sirens.

"The police are here, Thomas!" she shouted, but he was too enraged to stop his battering.

"I'll kill you, you bitch! You're dead! You're dead!"

"Stop! Police! Stop right there!" she heard yelled from outside. Footsteps hammered up the stairs, and she heard scuffling and shouting on the landing.

"They're here," she whispered into the receiver.

"Stay where you are. Wait until an officer identifies himself to you," the voice on the phone said.

It seemed an eon before a voice said, "Ma'am, I'm Officer Rodriguez. It's okay now. He's cuffed and my partner is taking him to the car."

Still trembling, she put down the phone and unlocked the dead bolt and chain of the ruined door. "Thank you," she managed to whisper. "Thank you. I'll file charges. I'll do whatever is needed. He meant to murder me, you know."

"Yes, ma'am. We'll take him down to the station and book him. Don't you worry about him hurting you."

The policeman left, and she slumped against the jamb, still clutching the candlestick in her hand.

"Olivia! Olivia!"

She glanced up to see Jackson bolting down the driveway bellowing her name. He tore up the steps two at a time and, when he reached her, gathered her into his arms.

"My God, are you all right? What happened? Who was that?"

"Thomas Fairchild. My ex-husband. He found me. He saw me on television, and he found me. God, I was so scared. He was going to murder me."

Rage flashed over Jackson's face, and he clutched her to him. "That sorry son of a bitch! I'll kill him if he ever comes near you again. You're *mine!*" He hugged her tighter. "You're *mine,* and I won't let him touch you!"

Olivia's spine stiffened as fury shot over her. "Don't you dare say that! Don't you dare. I'm not *yours!* I'm not his, and I'm not yours. I belong to no man." She struggled from his grip. "Get your hands off me!"

He tried to gather her into his arms again. "Olivia, darlin', calm down."

Flailing her hands and slapping at him, she elbowed her way out of his hold. "Don't you *darlin'* me. And I'm perfectly calm. Go away. Just go away!"

"Sugar, I'm not leaving while you're in this state. Let me take care of you."

"Dammit, don't you hear me?" she screamed. "Go away! I don't want you here. I don't need any man to take care of me. I can take care of myself. Go away!"

Jackson looked hurt, but she was too raw and too distraught to worry about his feelings. She was in survival mode and teetering on the edge.

He turned and walked slowly down the stairs. A

crowd of neighbors had gathered and were watching the spectacle, but she didn't care.

She went inside and slammed what was left of her door, then threw herself on her bed and wept. She cried and cursed every man who had tried to control her and humiliate her, beating her fist on the mattress and venting her anger and her fear.

When the well of tears was empty and her anger and fear had dissipated, she rolled over onto her back and stared at the ceiling. Maybe she had overreacted with Jackson, but his words had shaken her. Twice now she'd witnessed his fury. Jackson Crow had a temper.

And his proclamation that she was *his* had pierced her heart and struck at her most vulnerable spot. What was it about her that made the men in her life so possessive? What made them think that they could declare ownership of her as if she were no more than a pet dog?

Never again would she allow this. Never again. Not with Jackson, not with anyone. Good thing that she saw this side of him now rather than sometime in the future. She knew the pattern.

Her first impulse was to pack and leave, move far away from Jackson, abandon her quarters now that Thomas knew where to find her. But, then again, that had always been her custom. Flee.

Not this time. This time she was staying. She loved her job; she loved Austin. She was almost finished with her dissertation. She refused to let any man ruin her life again. She was going to live life on her own terms.

Rising, Olivia washed her face and called JoAnna.

She would spend a few days with her friend until her door was repaired and until she could be sure that Thomas wouldn't bother her again.

She wasn't leaving Austin.

Fourteen

Jackson hadn't wanted to leave Olivia, but she had been so upset, he hadn't known what else to do. He'd tried to call Tessa, but the Jurneys weren't home. He would have called JoAnna, but he didn't know her phone number, and he couldn't find it in the directory. He didn't want to phone Irish, in her condition, and get her all upset. He did the only thing he knew to do. He called his mother.

Wise woman, his mother.

She told him to make sure Olivia was safe from her ex-husband and to give her some time. "Let her know that you care and that you're there for her, but don't push. And for goodness sakes, don't start beating your chest and making all those he-man noises. It won't help."

"Yes, ma'am."

"Jackson, your father and I really like Olivia. We think you've hit another jackpot with her."

He grinned. "Yes, ma'am. My luck seems to be holding. I love you, Mama."

"I love you, too, son. And I have a feeling that things will work out between you and Olivia. You seem perfect together."

After he hung up, he considered what he could do to make sure that Olivia was safe. The number-one thing was to make sure her ex-husband stayed locked up and far away from Olivia.

He picked up the phone again and called the person he knew with the most political clout—Mitch. He briefly explained the situation and asked if he could help.

"As governor, I can't do much directly," Mitch said, "but the chief of police owes me a couple of favors. Let me call George and find out what's going on. I'll get back to you."

For an hour Jackson tried to read the material for the upcoming commission hearings, but his heart wasn't in it. Mostly he paced, waiting for Mitch's call.

When the phone rang, he eagerly snatched it up. Instead of Mitch, Tessa was on the line, asking what had happened. "I had a cryptic message from Olivia, telling me about the break-in and that she was going to stay with a friend. Is she there?"

"No, I believe that she's with a girlfriend, Tessa, and I'm glad to know that she's safe." He filled her in with the details, as much as he knew. He even told her about Olivia's reaction to his trying to help.

Tessa's advice was almost the same as his mother's.

"I have the governor looking into things—but for gosh sakes don't let Olivia know that. And I'll call a carpenter to fix the door."

"Forget the door," Tessa said. "Ed and Bill will take care of it. See that she's safe, Jackson. She's been terrified by that man for so long it's almost ruined her life. Be patient with her."

"I will."

Half an hour later Mitch called. "Did you know that Thomas Fairchild is a federal judge in California?"

"A *judge?* My God."

"Yep. Would you believe Olivia called me for help not fifteen minutes after we talked?"

"I hope you didn't tell her that I'd called you."

"Sorry. I did. I didn't realize it was a secret."

Jackson groaned. Now she was really going to be hacked at him. "What's going on?"

"I found out that Fairchild was about to worm his way out of jail in a few hours when George got involved. The most he can do is hold him for twenty-four hours, then the bastard can post bail and be out. Olivia can get a restraining order, but they don't always do much good. I have a better idea."

"Which is?"

"Harlon Swain and I are going to go visit Fairchild in jail." Harlon Swain was also a federal judge, one with many years of service, who had the ear of the powers that be in Washington as well as a supremely commanding voice and presence. He was a male version of the late Barbara Jordan.

"We're going to see if we can put the fear of God and Texas in this fellow," Mitch said. "Ride him out of town on a rail, so to speak."

"Think it will work?"

Mitch laughed. "You've got me, but Harlon seems to think it will. He's asked around, and from what he's found out about Fairchild, and from what Olivia told me, appearances are important to him. So is his judgeship. We can escort him to the airport and send him back to California with the charges dropped, or we can pursue the matter and get him thrown off the bench. If we let him off, he has to swear that he'll get some psychological help and never set foot in Texas again."

"Do it."

"Say, buddy, what's going on with you and Olivia? She was colder than a marble gravestone when I mentioned your name. Are things off with y'all?"

"Don't go getting any ideas, Mitch. She's still—spoken for." Damn, he'd almost said "mine." He was going to have to erase that word from his vocabulary. "Keep me posted, will you? And don't mention to Olivia that we talked. She gets pissed if she thinks somebody is interfering in her business."

Now, Jackson thought, if he could just manage to be patient.

He tried his dead-level best for the next few days. From what Mitch told him, he and Harlon had put on quite a show, and Fairchild had taken the first plane back to California. The bastard jumped on the chance to keep his job and his good name. Olivia was rid of him for good.

And she was back at her apartment. The door was

fixed, and he saw her coming and going, but she wouldn't take his calls or return his messages.

He sent her flowers and cards every day. Hell, he even had dinner delivered to her door every night with a note to call if she needed someone to share it with.

Nothing. *Nada.* Zip.

Not even a polite thank-you note.

Patience, his mother warned.

He muttered—and waited.

Olivia could ignore the prime rib, the lobster, the fillet of sole and chicken Florentine, each with a bottle of the finest wine, but when she opened the latest dinner box, she almost wept. Inside were four hotdogs with mustard, chili and cheese, and a big bag of potato chips. Instead of wine, there was a six-pack of Jackson's favorite beer. The note said: ''Call me, darlin'. I'm starving to death.''

She had tried to cut Jackson from her life, told herself that she was crazy to make herself vulnerable to a man again. Trouble was, she loved Jackson Crow, plain and simple.

She freely admitted that she'd overreacted to him the day of the break-in, but she'd been so keyed up that she couldn't help it. Now that her life belonged to her again and she had time to think rationally, she realized that Jackson was nothing like Thomas or her father. Protective? Absolutely. Hadn't he called Mitch to help her even before she thought of it? But manipulative and domineering? No.

And, darn it, she missed him something awful.

Picking up her phone, she punched in the familiar number.

Jackson answered on the first ring.

"Want to come over for a hotdog?" she asked.

"Damned right. I'm on my way."

He didn't even say goodbye, just hung up. From her kitchen window, she saw him charging out the courtyard gate, dragging a shirt over his head. She laughed. He was barefoot, and it was cold outside.

She heard his feet hit the stairs and in three seconds he was knocking on her door. When she opened it, he was leaning casually against the jamb, grinning in that delightfully endearing way of his.

"Come in," she said, resisting the urge to throw her arms around him and kiss him senseless. "Want a beer?"

"Don't mind if I do." Thumbs hooked in the belt of his jeans, he sauntered in.

"Aren't your feet cold?"

He looked down and, as if noticing for the first time that he was barefoot, wiggled his toes. "Damn! And I was trying to be so cool."

She laughed. "You are cool, Jackson Crow. Supercool. Or is it hot?" Unable to resist any longer, she put her arms around his neck and pulled him to her.

He didn't need any urging. His lips met hers in a kiss that made her knees sag.

He kissed her eyes and her cheeks and nuzzled his way under her chin. "Oh, darlin', I've been out of my mind. I love you so much."

"I love you, Jackson."

"Do you mean it? Honest to God?"

She smiled. "I do. I've missed you, too."

"Promise that you'll marry me, darlin', and put me out of my misery."

He reached for her lips again, but she pushed him away and took his face in her hands. "Jackson, I can't promise you that. I'm not ready to make that kind of commitment again. I may never be. There's so much that you don't know about me, about the kind of life I've had."

Leading her to the sofa, he sat down and pulled her into his lap. "Tell me. Tell me everything."

She did. She told him everything about her father's abuse of her mother, then of her brother and her, about her college fiancé's abuse, about her ex-husband's abuse. She related every ugly bit of the story.

Jackson closed his eyes during parts of the account, and she could see the muscles in his jaw moving as he controlled his anger, but he didn't say a word until she was finished. He only held her close and stroked her.

"So now do you see why I'm anxious about relationships?" she asked quietly. "It's not that I don't love you, Jackson. It's just that I'm...very wary."

"I'll wait."

"Jackson, I may never be ready to get married again. You should know that."

"Olivia, I love you with all my heart and soul. I'll wait. And in the meantime I'll settle for what I can get. You've brought joy into my life beyond measure." He smiled and traced her lips. "And you've brought colors that opened up a new world to me and changed the way I perceive everything, but the only color that's worth a damn is the color of your name." He kissed her deeply. "I'll wait."

Epilogue

The roadsides were a blanket of blue as Texas bluebonnets bloomed in profusion. Here and there along the highway to Dallas were patches of orange Indian paintbrush, pink evening primrose and other breathtaking spring wildflowers.

Olivia and Jackson were on their way to see Irish and Kyle's new son. Joshua had been born three days before, and mother and son were doing fine.

"Kyle sounded like he was about to pass out," Jackson had told Olivia after the call came, "but Irish and the baby are doing great. Seven pounds, nine ounces and gorgeous."

Olivia was anxious to see her friend. They talked weekly and had visited again at Christmas, but she could hardly wait to see that adorable baby.

She settled back, content to be with Jackson as he

drove. In the months they had been together, she'd learned a great deal about him. He was totally different from her father and Thomas. He had a temper, yes, but his anger was never directed against her. Jackson was a strong man with strong opinions, and he was very protective of her, sometimes overly so, but she knew for certain that he would never hurt her. Hadn't she deliberately provoked him several times to prove it to herself?

Every day she grew more and more sure that she was ready to commit to a permanent relationship. Instead of making her shudder, the notion filled her with warmth. She did adore the man. She smiled. And he was such a hottie.

After what seemed forever, they arrived in Dallas and went directly to Irish and Kyle's home. All the clan had gathered, even Jackson's sister, Congresswoman Ellen Crow O'Hara and her husband were there. Only Kyle's brother Smith was missing. He hadn't shown up at Christmas, either.

"I don't know what's the matter with that boy," Cherokee Pete said. "I miss him like the dickens."

"So do I," Sarah Rutledge said. "I wish he was here to see his new nephew and my new grandson. Isn't he beautiful?" she asked, folding back the blanket for Olivia and Jackson to get a better view of the bundle she held.

"He's precious," Olivia said. "May I hold him?"

Sarah transferred the baby to her, and as Olivia held him in her arms, a flow of maternal tenderness stole over her. "How wonderful to create this little soul." She smiled up at Jackson. "Why don't we have a little one like this?"

"I'm willing. But only if you'll marry me." He brushed her cheek with his knuckle, love shining from his eyes.

"I will."

"Do you really mean it, darlin'?"

She nodded. "Yes."

Folks could hear his whoop all the way to Austin.

* * * * *